D0560418

BLESSINGS OF
THE HEART

BLESSINGS OF THE HEART

Jane McBride Choate

THORNDIKE
CHIVERS

This Large Print edition is published by Thorndike Press®, Waterville, Maine USA and by BBC Audiobooks Ltd, Bath, England.

Published in 2006 in the U.S. by arrangement with Jane McBride Choate.

Published in 2006 in the U.K. by arrangement with the author.

U.S. Hardcover   0-7862-8807-8   (Candlelight)
U.K. Hardcover 10: 1 4056 3852 4   (Chivers Large Print)
U.K. Hardcover 13: 978 1 4056 3852 4
U.K. Softcover   10: 1 4056 3853 2   (Camden Large Print)
U.K. Softcover   13: 978 1 4056 3853 1

The text of this Large Print edition is unabridged.
Other aspects of the book may vary from the original edition.

Set in 16 pt. Plantin.

Printed in the United States on permanent paper.

British Library Cataloguing-in-Publication Data available

Library of Congress Cataloging-in-Publication Data

Choate, Jane McBride.
    Blessings of the heart / by Jane McBride Choate.
        p. cm. — (Thorndike Press large print candlelight)
      ISBN 0-7862-8807-8 (lg. print : hc : alk. paper)
      1. Large type books.   I. Title.   II. Series: Thorndike
    Press large print Candlelight series.
    PS3553.H575B57 2006
      813'.54—dc22   2006009727

To my father,
the inspiration for this book

Chapter One

Sam hitched the headband higher on his forehead. One more mile before he could call it quits. He swiped at his sweat-sheened face with the back of his hand.

Admit it, Hastings, he told himself in disgust. *You're out of shape.* Too much time spent campaigning and not enough working out had taken their toll.

He'd signed up to run five miles for a benefit to raise money for the community's homeless. And he intended to meet his goal . . . if only his lungs held out.

The sound of feet slapping the pavement behind him signaled that he was no longer alone.

"Hi." The woman now keeping pace with him was young, probably no older than twenty-five or so. "I'm Carla Stevens."

"Sam Hastings," he panted out between breaths. He glanced at her with a certain amount of resentment. She wasn't even breathing hard.

"I know."

"You do?"

"Uh-huh." She smiled. "See you after the race." She jogged ahead, her steady pace quickly outstripping his own.

"Yeah," he called after her. He watched her, liking the way she moved — with an easy grace that made his own efforts seem heavy and labored.

He gritted his teeth and geared himself up for the last mile. He'd make it. He had to. He could see the headlines now if he didn't finish: *City Council Hopeful Passes Out on Last Mile of Charity Race.*

Easy goes it, he reminded himself. *The race belongs not to the swift but to the* . . . He couldn't remember the end of the proverb and decided it didn't matter. He concentrated on putting one foot in front of the other.

"Number fifty-four," a race official announced as Sam crossed the finish line.

"Thanks," he said, accepting a glass of juice a volunteer handed him. He swallowed it in one gulp and wished he had another.

"Here," a familiar voice said. "You look like you need this."

He looked up to find the pretty lady who had passed him earlier holding a glass of juice.

"Thanks."

8

"You're welcome." She pointed to a shaded area. "Would you like to rest? I don't know about you, but I'm bushed."

She sank down on the yellowed grass and gestured for him to do the same. He propped himself against the trunk of a maple tree, its branches forging a crimson canopy overhead.

She didn't look bushed, Sam thought. She was probably just being kind. At the moment, he felt every one of his thirty-two years . . . and then some.

"I've been wanting to talk with you, Mr. Hastings. I need your help."

He suppressed a groan and a twinge of disappointment. *Here it comes.* Since he'd announced that he was running for City Council, people had been crawling out of the woodwork, wanting things from him. He wasn't even on the council yet, but the requests still kept coming.

"What can I do for you, Ms. Stevens?" he asked, not bothering to hide the resignation in his voice.

"It's about the benefit today."

"What about it?"

"You know that it's to raise money for a community home for the city's homeless population."

He nodded.

"We're about halfway to our goal —"

He held up a hand. "Just a minute. Who's 'we'?"

"Everyone Deserves a Home, the group that sponsored the race."

"You're a volunteer?"

She shook her head. "I'm one of the founders."

That explained a lot. "If you'll come by my office, I'll be happy to write a check for you."

"Thanks, but that's not what I want."

Since when did a representative from a charity turn down money? His interest piqued, he asked, "What do you want?"

"I want you to visit one of the welfare apartments with me, see what the conditions are like, then make the public aware of them." Her words came out in a rush, as if the feeling behind them couldn't be contained a moment longer. "If someone like you speaks out, people will listen."

Sam thought of the apathy he'd encountered since declaring his candidacy. The lady was incredibly naive if she thought he could do anything. "You really think one person's going to make a difference?"

"One person . . . one voice . . . can always make a difference." She twisted her hands in her lap. "You're a public figure,

Mr. Hastings. If you visit one of these apartments, then others will too. If people know — understand — just how awful these places are, they'll be more willing to support the home we want to build. We need an endorsement from a public figure." She paused, looking straight at him, her clear blue eyes challenging him to accept.

"Look, Ms. Stevens, I have at least a dozen requests each day to support one cause or another. What makes yours so special?"

"Because everyone deserves a decent place to live." She stood and brushed grass from her running shorts. "Obviously, that means nothing to someone like you, but it does to me."

He grabbed her arm. "What do you mean, someone like me?"

"Samuel Hastings — son of Richard and Estelle Hastings, president of Hastings Architecture. Member of the Chamber of Commerce. Candidate for City Council."

"So you know my background. What about it?"

"Have you ever been hungry, Mr. Hastings? Have you ever had to sleep on the streets in the middle of winter? Or go to a shelter?"

"No, but —"

She freed her arm. "I didn't think so. I'm sorry I wasted your time." She walked away without a backward glance.

Sam stared after her, aware that he'd been evaluated and found wanting. She'd neatly tagged him as rich, pampered, and spoiled. It wasn't the first time such labels had been attached to his name, and it wouldn't be the last. He'd decided a long time ago he wouldn't let it bother him.

But the memory of the cool contempt in her eyes stayed with him for the rest of the day.

Well, I've blown it this time, Carla berated herself in exasperation as she walked away.

She'd led with her heart instead of her head. And in doing so, she'd alienated the one man who might have been willing to help.

When she'd read Sam Hastings' name on the list of participants in the race, she'd seized upon it as an opportunity to enlist his support for the community home that her group wanted to build.

She'd attended several debates between Hastings and his opponent for the City Council of Saratoga, New York. He'd impressed her as a man who backed up what he said with action. When she heard him speak about wanting to help the city's homeless, she thought she'd found someone who believed as she did.

But, as always, when she felt passionately about something, she'd plunged in heart-first without thinking the matter through. She didn't blame him — entirely — for refusing her request.

A cloud of failure settled over her spirits as she acknowledged that she was also at least partially to blame. She'd come on too strong, too fast. But that didn't excuse his callousness in turning her down flat, she thought with a return of anger.

Just as quickly as the anger appeared, it dissolved. She'd learned years ago that anger didn't solve problems; it created them. But still she couldn't help being disappointed that she'd misread him so completely.

She'd thought he was different from other politicians. Meeting him, talking with him, had only strengthened that impression. But she'd been wrong. It wasn't the first time she'd misjudged a man.

The phone hadn't stopped ringing since he'd stepped into his office at eight the next morning. By noon, Sam felt he would need to have the phone surgically removed from his ear. He buzzed his secretary Sarah on the intercom. "Hold my calls."

"Until when?"

He looked at his desk, piled high with yesterday's mail, mock-ups for campaign ads, and heaven knew what else.

"Until I tell you differently."

"Sure thing, Boss."

Sam smiled as he switched off the intercom. Sarah had been with him from the beginning, a holdover from the first year of business. She'd stuck it out through the slim years when he didn't know if Hastings Architecture was going to sink or swim.

He didn't know what he'd do without her; he didn't want to find out. If he won the election, he was going to depend upon her more than ever. She knew more about the business than anyone else in the company, including him.

He pulled out a sample of a campaign brochure that his manager, Jerry Ross, had designed. Sam groaned as he read the text extolling his virtues and military record. And the picture of him in uniform — where had Jerry come up with that? It had to be at least ten years old.

Sam scrawled one word across the pamphlet. *No.*

He grinned briefly. Jerry would have a fit, but that couldn't be helped. He hadn't been altogether certain about entering the race for City Council, but since he had, he was determined to run his campaign as he ran his company: no false promises, only honest hard work.

Methodically, he worked his way through the remaining things on his desk. When he pushed back his chair a couple of hours later, he let out a sigh of satisfaction.

Idly, he picked up the phone book and flipped through it until he came to the S's. He ran his finger down the lists of names until he found the one he was looking for. *Stevens, C.*

Her accusations had bothered him more than he cared to admit — primarily because he feared they might be true. He hadn't experienced hunger or any of the other things she'd named. A guilty twinge nagged at his conscience. Perhaps he'd been too quick to dismiss her and her request.

Before he could talk himself out of it, he punched out her number. "Ms. Stevens? It's Sam Hastings. I wonder if you'd have lunch with me tomorrow."

Sam was smiling as he hung up the phone a few minutes later. Carla Stevens had class, he decided. He didn't expect, and certainly didn't deserve, her graciousness in accepting his apology.

He found himself looking forward to a lunch date for the first time in a long time.

He was nearly late when he entered the restaurant the following day. A glance around confirmed Carla wasn't there yet either.

A waiter showed him to his table. He heard a slight stir and looked up to see what had caused it. A nun — no, a minister — was walking toward him.

He took a closer look. It was. . . . He shook his head. It couldn't be. But it was.

Carla.

"Am I late?" she asked, her voice a trifle breathless.

"No." He stood and pulled out a chair for her.

"You were staring."

"Was I? I'm sorry." Even so, he couldn't drag his gaze away from the gray minister's garb.

"You didn't know, did you?" She touched the white collar that encircled her neck. "About this."

"You could say that."

"I should have told you on the phone."

"Why didn't you?"

16

"I was afraid you'd take back your invitation. A lot of people are uncomfortable around a minister — especially a minister who also happens to be a woman."

Her frankness disarmed him, as did the clear navy-blue eyes staring back at him.

"Do you have a problem with it?" she asked.

"I don't know," he said honestly. "I've never known a lady minister before."

"If it makes you feel any better, just pretend that I'm not wearing a white collar. I'm a woman."

He let his gaze linger on the dark hair framing her face with soft curls. Her lips were full and bare of lipstick. "You'll get no argument from me there."

Color smudged Carla's cheeks.

Sam smiled, enchanted. When was the last time he'd seen a woman blush? "I'm sorry. I didn't mean to embarrass you."

A waiter appeared.

The color heightened in her cheeks. "I . . . you . . . shall we order?"

After they'd placed their orders, Sam asked, "How did a minister become involved with a 10K race?"

"Just because I'm a minister doesn't mean I'm dead. I have to admit I wasn't sold on the idea at first. But the group I work with, Everyone Deserves a Home, decided it would be a great money-maker. And it was." She grinned. "Thanks to you and all the others who entered."

"Tell me about your group."

She studied him frankly.

Sam was surprised to find himself fighting the urge to squirm under her scrutiny. Not many people had that effect on him. Of course, not many people looked him straight in the eye with the unblinking gaze Carla was subjecting him to now.

"Just remember," she warned, "you asked."

He sat back, prepared to listen.

She leaned forward. "We want to help people get off the streets and into decent housing. The money from the race and other fund-raising projects will go to build a community home."

"What's a community home?"

"A stopgap for people who have nowhere else to go. It'll have everything. There'll be private apartments for families, job training for teenagers, classes on how to write a resume. . . ."

All the while she talked, Sam watched her. She wasn't beautiful, not in the accepted sense of perfect features, but her eyes held compassion and understanding and a warmth that drew him even as he told himself he should stay away.

She flushed. "I'm sorry. I tend to rattle on when I get started on this."

"Don't apologize. I like listening to you."

Carla looked uncertain, but he smiled encouragingly and soon the words were tumbling out again. Her face grew animated as she used her hands to emphasize a point.

Sam asked questions, wanting to keep her talking. Her voice, low and musical, worked its own special magic, and he let it spread its warmth over him. He hadn't realized how edgy he'd been until he felt the tension melt away under the soft cadence of her voice.

When lunch arrived, they were still talking. Sam was trying to understand how people ended up on the streets and Carla was challenging his preconceived ideas.

The lunch dishes were cleared, the bill presented, and still they continued to talk. A discreet cough from the waiter reminded Sam that they needed to vacate the table.

"I owe you an apology for yesterday," he said as he stood and placed some bills on the table.

"We already took care of that on the phone," she reminded him.

"I was rude. Let me make it up to you."

She looked ready to refuse.

"Please."

He watched as doubt and then something else flitted across her face. That something else caused her lips to twitch.

"If you really want to make it up to me, take a drive with me."

"A drive?"

"You said you owed me. I'm collecting."

"Where?"

"You'll see."

Outside the restaurant, she led him to a beat-up compact sporting a bumper sticker that read, *Don't laugh. It's paid for.*

Sam admired her style. She didn't apologize for her car; instead, she patted it fondly.

"This is Emma."

"Emma?"

"After my grandmother, Emma Jane Wentworth."

"You named a car after your grandmother?"

"Sure. Why not?"

"How does she feel about it?"

"Gram's been dead for more than ten years, but I think she'd have been pleased. She and my car are a lot alike — small and feisty."

Sam couldn't help the low rumble that started somewhere in his chest and erupted into a gust of laughter. "I have a feeling I would have liked your grandmother."

"She'd have liked you too."

He didn't know why the compliment pleased him so much. Maybe because he sensed Carla wasn't the type to say things she didn't mean. He turned his attention back to the car and eyed it dubiously.

"Why don't we take mine? It's —" He started to say more reliable, and said instead, "— bigger."

She grinned. "Don't worry. You won't hurt Emma's feelings. But I don't think it's a good idea to take your car. Not where we're going."

"Just where *are* we going?"

"Don't you trust me?" she asked, her smile doing funny things to his insides. "A woman of the cloth?"

He laughed, liking Carla Stevens more and more. She was totally without pretensions, a rarity in the people he normally associated with.

Sam folded himself into the car, grimacing as he bent his long legs to fit the small contours. Carla pushed the seat back as far as it would go, but even so his knees

21

all but touched his chin. He looked at her, saw the merriment in her eyes, and felt himself responding to it. He couldn't remember the last time he'd enjoyed himself so much.

His laughter died when he realized she was heading into one of the city's roughest areas. "Just where is it you're taking me?"

"You're about to see how the other half lives."

So that was it. Well, he had to hand it to her — the lady didn't quit.

She parked her car in front of a shabby apartment building with the unlikely name of Royal Arms and turned to him. "Are you up to a tour?"

He read the challenge in her eyes. "It's your show. Lead the way." After he helped her out, he looked at the graffiti-scarred building. His feet crunched over cracked glass which littered the sidewalk.

Carla walked up to a group of men loitering on the crumbling cement stairs.

"Hiya, Minister lady," one said, his lips pulled back over a toothless grin.

"Hi yourself, George. Brought a friend with me today. All right if I take him inside?"

George waved a hand. "Be sure to show him the Presidential Suite." He cackled, obviously pleased with his own joke.

Assorted guffaws followed as the men poked one another in the ribs.

"That's a good one, George," a grizzled man with yellowed teeth said. "The Presidential Suite."

"I'll see you later," Carla said, and took Sam inside.

Inside the lobby, they picked their way around trash cans, the garbage spilling onto the floor. She led him up a stairway, showing him where to step so that the stairs didn't collapse beneath his weight.

Sam didn't bother to ask how she knew where to step. It was obvious she was a frequent visitor here. The idea bothered him as he remembered the rundown area of town where the apartments were located.

He wasn't usually given to chauvinistic tendencies, but he was suddenly afraid for Carla. He didn't want her hurt. He didn't bother to question the fact that he had no right to feel protective toward this woman whom he'd met only yesterday.

She stopped outside apartment number seventeen and pushed on the door. It creaked on its hinges as it groaned its way open. "This one's empty, but it won't be for long. There's always a waiting list."

Sam had prepared himself to expect the

worst, but he couldn't contain his hiss of revulsion as he looked around the apartment. He'd visited tenements before, but he'd never seen squalor like that which met his gaze now.

Obscene words covered the walls. Crudely cut pieces of cardboard shielded the windows, scant protection against the wind that wailed outside.

Carla pointed to the walls where the paint had peeled away. "Do you know what lead poisoning does to children?"

She didn't give him an opportunity to answer, but led him into the bathroom, carefully stepping over broken pieces of glass. Rust coated the fixtures, the linoleum floor was cracked, and backed-up plumbing created a stench that wouldn't quit.

"You've made your point, Reverend," he said. "Let's get out of here."

"Not yet."

He followed her out of the apartment and down a hallway where she stopped to knock at a door.

When no one answered it, she called, "Mona, it's me, Carla."

The door inched open, and a pair of brown eyes peered out.

Carla knelt so that she was at eye level

with the little girl. "Hi, Punkin. Is your mommy home?"

"In here, Reverend Stevens," a tired voice called.

Sam followed her inside and saw a woman sprawled under the kitchen sink.

"I'm trying to fix the sink," she said. "I'll just be a minute." After twisting a wrench back and forth, she said, "Could you turn on the water?"

Carla turned the faucet.

"It's not leaking," the woman said jubilantly.

She crawled from under the sink, stood, and wiped her hands on her jeans. "Sorry about that. It's been leaking for the last week. I got tired of waiting for Mr. Do-Nothing to fix it, so I did it myself."

"Mr. Do-Nothing?" Sam repeated.

"The landlord," Carla said. "Mona Freeman, meet Sam Hastings."

Sam held out his hand. After a moment's hesitation, the young woman put her hand inside his.

"Please to meet you, Mr. Hastings," she said. "Mary, say hi to the Reverend and her friend."

The little girl clung to her mother's leg. "Hi, Reverend." She didn't look at Sam.

He hunkered down to her level. "Hi, Mary. My name's Sam."

She scooted behind her mother.

"I'm sorry," Mona apologized. "She's not comfortable with men."

"Mona," Carla said, "I brought Sam by so that he could see firsthand what the Royal Arms is like."

Mona stepped back. "Be my guest."

Self-consciously, Sam looked around. The apartment was clean and tidy, but bore the same evidence of decay and neglect as the first.

Mona Freeman obviously worked hard to make the shabby apartment into a home. Handmade pillows were plumped over the sagging sofa; plants enlivened bleak corners; a child's artwork hung on the walls.

But nothing could disguise the ripped carpet, peeling walls, and broken windows.

He caught his toe on the corner of the kitchen linoleum. Only his quick reflexes kept him from falling.

Mona rushed forward. "Are you all right?"

"Fine," he said, stepping around the torn spot. "How long has the floor been ripped?"

"Since last year. I've tried to fix it, but it just pops right back up."

"The landlord refuses to do anything about it?"

She rolled her eyes.

Sam looked at Carla, who nodded. She fished in her purse and handed Mary a piece of candy. "Thanks for letting us come in, Mona. We need to be going now."

Once more, Sam offered his hand to Mona. "Thank you, Ms. Freeman. I've enjoyed meeting you and your little girl."

By mutual consent, Carla and Sam stopped at the landing and looked out a window. Steel bars obstructed their view. "Why do they stay?"

"They don't have anywhere else to go." Carla paused, as though weighing how much to tell him. "You probably guessed that Mona's a single mother."

"What happened to Mary's father?"

"Mona left him when he started beating up on Mary."

Sam's lips tightened, but he didn't say anything. He looked around, unable to keep the disgust from his voice. "There must be somewhere else they could go. Anywhere's better than this."

"You really don't understand, do you? It's this or the streets. A lot of people prefer the streets, especially those without families. Those who don't, stay here or somewhere like it."

Sam pulled out a checkbook and scrawled something.

"I hope this helps," he said, handing it to her.

Carla accepted the check, her eyes widening at the amount. "Thanks," she said, slipping it into her purse. "As you can see, we need all the help we can get."

"Do I hear a 'but' in there somewhere?"

She smiled. "You're very perceptive."

He skimmed his knuckles across her cheek. "Your face is very revealing."

"People forced to live here need a lot more than money, Sam."

"I realize —"

"I'm not sure you do. Most people think that if the people worked harder, they wouldn't be on the streets or forced to live in a dump like this."

"I didn't say that."

"You didn't have to."

"Am I so transparent?"

"Your reaction isn't unusual. Most people feel the same way until they see the reality of apartments like these. Until they see children with rat bites that won't heal. Until they see backed-up toilets and sinks whose only water is brown with rust. Until they see —" She broke off and flushed. "I'm sorry. I get carried away."

"I didn't mean —"

"Don't apologize. Just try to understand. These are decent people. Most of them have families. But they need jobs and self-respect. Mostly, they need homes. Not just a bed in a public shelter or a rattrap apartment like these." She laughed self-consciously. "I didn't mean to get on my soapbox again. It's just that —"

"Hey, it's okay. I like listening to you. You care about people. That's rare today."

"Not really."

"You're so naive you don't even realize how special that makes you."

"I stopped being naive six years ago when I took my vows. There's so much need —" She gestured around her. "— I decided I had to help. I couldn't sit in my office and write sermons while people were living like this. I started looking with my heart, instead of just my eyes. Try it, and you might see more than you ever imagined."

He looked at her and saw the commitment, the compassion that sparked her eyes. No, she'd never be able to sit back and simply wait for others to help. She'd be leading the crusade. He liked that about her. He liked *her*.

"Just how old are you, anyway?" he asked, remembering his earlier guess.

"Twenty-seven. Almost twenty-eight."

"You must have started right out of college."

"I always knew I wanted to be a minister. I pictured myself as one of the great missionaries, going to Africa and converting thousands." A faint smile rested on her lips. "Instead, I ended up here."

"Do you regret it?"

She looked thoughtful. "I used to think so but not anymore. This is where I want to be. Come on," she added, grabbing his hand. "I think you've had enough for today."

Sam couldn't help but agree.

They retraced their steps, again picking their way carefully down the stairway and through the lobby.

He gave a sheepish smile at the relieved breath he expelled when they were once more outside. "You've got yourself a convert. Just tell me what you want me to do."

"Start talking about what you've seen here. Tell your friends, your colleagues, anyone who'll listen, what it's like. Then maybe we'll get the support we need to build the community home."

"Done. Now it's my turn to ask a favor."

"Name it."

"Have dinner with me tomorrow night."

"That's the favor?"

He'd taken her by surprise. He could see it in her eyes and decided to press his advantage. "Please," he added, much as she had just hours before.

"I don't think —"

"If it'll make you feel any better, we can discuss the community home some more."

"All right . . . if you're sure."

"Oh, I'm sure."

Sam didn't try to analyze why being with Carla Stevens was so important. But he intended to find out.

Chapter Two

Back in her office at the rectory, Carla regretted her impulse in accepting Sam's invitation. A dozen times, she picked up the phone, intending to break the date. But something always stopped her.

Maybe it was the way he looked at her, as though he saw the woman inside the minister's garb. Maybe it was the way she felt when he held her hand. Maybe it was because he was by far the most attractive man she'd seen in a long time.

Whatever it was, she knew she couldn't deny the stirring inside her when she thought of him.

She pushed aside those feelings and concentrated on the papers in front of her. Everyone Deserves a Home had netted over five thousand dollars from the race. Combined with what was already in their treasury, they had enough to put a bid on some land.

It was up to her and the others on the site committee to start scouting out locations for the community home. Once they had a piece of land, they could start building.

She looked at Sam's check. It was more than generous; it also represented the differences between them. He saw money as the way to right what was wrong with the world; she knew it took more than that. Much more.

But he'd been genuinely distressed at the conditions at the Royal Arms. Maybe, just maybe, he could help them.

By the following evening as she looked through her limited wardrobe, Carla was certain she'd made a mistake. A date with Sam Hastings?

Anyone who'd ever read the society page was familiar with his name and his family. Every week, he was shown with a different woman, each more beautiful than the last. His mother was on the board of at least a dozen charities, his father president of the largest bank in the city.

She had to be out of her mind to go out with Sam. They had nothing in common.

Her hand settled on a blue dress, its simple lines lending it an air of sophistication she hoped would give her some much-needed confidence. She dressed quickly, annoyed by her uncharacteristic dithering.

Tonight wasn't a date, she reminded herself. It was an opportunity to enlist help for her group. But she couldn't control the tiny shiver of excitement that skittered down her spine as she brushed her hair.

Sam was punctual. His low whistle at her appearance was flattering. But then, a man like Sam would know how to make a woman feel special.

"You look great," he said.

"So do you."

In a charcoal suit, white shirt, and burgundy tie, he looked sensational.

His car wasn't what she'd expected. Instead of a Mercedes or BMW, he drove a pickup truck — a shiny red pickup.

"You look surprised," he said, helping her to climb inside.

"I am."

"Didn't they teach you in divinity school not to judge by appearances?"

She smiled. "You're right. And I'm sorry."

"We're through with apologizing, remember?"

"I remember," she said softly.

The restaurant probably catered to the rich and famous, Carla decided as Sam pulled up in front of what looked like a nineteenth-century mansion. Stately oaks and maples lined the driveway. A small stream wound its way through the grounds.

As he led her inside, she took in the quiet but tasteful decor. Victorian furniture was arranged in small clusters in the lobby, inviting patrons to relax and chat. A silver tea service was placed on an ornately carved sideboard.

In the dining room, white-coated waiters appeared discreetly and then disappeared just as discreetly. Crystal and china gleamed upon damask-covered tables. The whole atmosphere was one of wealth — understated but unmistakable wealth.

She ordered from a menu that had no prices listed. Her poached fish in wine sauce was excellent, but she barely tasted it.

"You're not enjoying yourself," Sam said.

"I am. It's just that. . . ." She let her words trail off, unwilling to continue.

"What?"

"I feel guilty."

"Why?"

"I'm not used to such extravagance. What you're spending on dinner tonight could feed a family for a week. Maybe more."

"I'll bet your mother used to make you clean your plate so the children in India wouldn't go hungry."

The smile slipped out despite her best efforts to remain serious. "As a matter of fact, she did."

"Mine did too. I never could figure out the correlation between my stomach and hungry kids overseas." He shook his head ruefully. "I guess your mom had better luck with you." His smile invited her to share his amusement.

But she couldn't respond to it this time. "It's different when you actually see hunger day after day. It becomes real to you and not just an article in the newspaper or a story on television."

"So you're not supposed to enjoy yourself because other people are hungry?"

"I'm sorry, Sam. I *am* having a good time. Honestly, I'm just not used to all this."

"You're an enigma, Carla Stevens. You look like you should be sipping tea with the rest of the society ladies, yet you spend your time running in charity races and visiting welfare apartments."

"I'm not an enigma. I'm just different than your usual date."

He cocked his head to one side. "What's my usual date?"

"She's very pretty, intelligent, and successful. She wears designer clothes, prefers sushi to steak, and drinks white wine. She works out at a fitness club and reads all the books on the *New York Times* best-seller list."

Sam frowned at the description. He didn't like what he heard; even less did he like acknowledging her accuracy. The lady was too perceptive by half.

"How'd I do?" she prompted.

"Not bad," he admitted with a rueful laugh. "Not bad at all."

"You don't like being predictable."

He thought about it. She was right — again. He didn't like being predictable. But then Carla was showing him a lot of things about himself, not all of them pleasant.

He took her hand across the table and studied it. It was small, like the woman herself. It was also capable-looking, the skin slightly roughened as though she were accustomed to hard work. It intrigued him. *She* intrigued him.

"What about your personal life?" he asked. "You do have a personal life, don't you?"

"Of course I do. I read to preschoolers at the local library, I lead a book club for the teenagers in the church, and once a week I work at the hospital in the neonatal unit."

He watched as her eyes softened at this. "You're a nurse too?"

She smiled, shaking her head. "No. I hold the preemies . . . the babies who can't be taken home because they were born too soon."

"Did you hear what you just told me?" He didn't wait for her answer. "You volunteer at the library, at the school, at the hospital. What do you do for *you?* What do you do for Carla, the woman?"

"It's you who doesn't understand. I do all those things for myself. Because I enjoy them. If I didn't, I wouldn't do them."

"Wouldn't you?" he asked, still holding her hand. It tensed inside his.

"Of course not."

But her words lacked conviction. Did she do those things because she enjoyed them or were they just a way to fill the empty hours? She pushed away the thought. Her hours weren't empty, far from it. They were filled to capacity.

"Hey, I didn't mean to upset you," Sam said.

"You didn't." She felt Sam's speculative gaze on her, but she didn't elaborate. Right now, she needed time to think. Sam's nearness wasn't helping. It wasn't helping at all.

"Have dinner with me Friday night," he said, drawing her back to the present.

She laughed. "You didn't mean to say that."

"Yes, I did."

She shook her head. "You asked me out tonight as an experiment."

He frowned. "An experiment?"

"Yes. You wanted to see what being with a lady minister was like. Would she spout Bible verses all evening and try to convert you? Does she wear her minister outfit all the time or does she dress like a real woman occasionally?"

A reluctant laugh escaped before he could stifle it. "You missed your calling. You should have been a mind reader."

"No, Sam," she said gently. "I found my calling."

That sobered him. "I'm sorry. I didn't mean to tease you."

Her fingers rested lightly on his arm. "I know."

"I still want to see you again. Have dinner with me, Carla. I'll take you somewhere fun, somewhere you don't have to worry about how much it costs."

"Not this time." She smiled to soften the refusal. "It's my turn to treat. If you come to my house, I'll cook dinner for you."

"A home-cooked meal?" The idea was more appealing than he believed possible.

"That's right."

"I didn't figure women cooked anymore."

"This one does. I have to if I want to eat. Ministers don't rate big salaries."

"May I bring something? Wine or dessert?"

"Dessert would be great."

"It's a date."

"A date?" She looked as if she were testing the idea. "I guess it is."

Sam took her home and left her at the door . . . without kissing her good night. Carla had been right. He had asked her out as an experiment, to prove to himself that she wasn't his type of woman.

Only it had backfired. The evening had made him want to spend more time with her, to get to know her better.

Carla thought of little else but the upcoming date for the next two days. As she worked on Sunday's sermon, she saw Sam's face. Leading her Bible study group, she thought of Sam. As she read to the preschoolers at the library, she wondered if Sam liked children.

In fact, Sam was occupying far too much

of her thinking and attention, and she resolved to push him out of her mind. But that was easier said than done.

Especially when he called up Thursday to remind her of their date on Friday, his deep voice a calm anchor in the midst of a hectic day. Especially when he sent a bouquet of golden mums delivered to her office at the church. Especially when she didn't *want* to stop thinking about him.

She was very much afraid that Sam Hastings was in her thoughts to stay. The only question was, did she want to let him in her life?

Everything that could go wrong on Friday managed to do so — and then some. Carla's plans of a leisurely day to prepare dinner and then get herself ready evaporated under a series of emergencies.

First, the ancient pipes in the women's rest room of the church burst, flooding into the adjacent nursery. She spent the morning mopping up gallons of water and waiting for the plumber to arrive.

Just as she was finishing up, a teenage girl showed up at the church, claiming she was running away from home. Carla spent the next hour listening to the girl rail against the unfairness of her parents. A call to the parents and another hour of counseling followed, with the result that the girl and her parents returned home together with the promise to start talking and listening to each other.

After returning home, Carla browned the pot roast and put it into a Crockpot when the phone rang again.

What now? she asked herself.

It was the Lindquists, a young couple with a new baby, desperate to find a baby-sitter so that they could have an evening for themselves. Steve and Marianne Lindquist had had a rough time of it lately. Steve, a carpenter, had recently lost his job, and was trying to support the family on odd jobs. At home with a new baby and no car, Marianne struggled to find time for herself.

Sam would understand, Carla told herself. It wasn't as if this was a real date. It was only two people having dinner together . . . a dinner she still had to cook.

After the Lindquists dropped Emilie off, Carla settled the baby down for a nap. She watched as Emilie hiked her little bottom in the air and began sucking on her thumb. For a moment, Carla let her imagination take hold, pretending Emilie was hers. She loved children and wanted a dozen of her own.

After checking the time, she gave up thoughts of the long bath she'd planned and opted for a quick shower before preparing the remainder of the dinner.

The buzz of the doorbell an hour later woke Emilie from her nap. Carla picked up the baby, quieting her with soft words, then went to answer the door.

She stifled a chuckle at the bemused look on Sam's face as he took in the sight of her holding Emilie.

"I'm sorry," she said, shifting Emilie in her arms. "I'm running a little late. Some friends asked if I'd tend Emilie for them tonight. They haven't had a night out since she was born."

Carla led Sam into the living room and gestured toward the overstuffed sofa. She wished she'd remembered to place a pillow over the torn spot in the upholstery. The sofa had been a gift of sorts from a family in the church who had been transferred to another city.

In fact, that's how she'd acquired most of her furniture — castoffs, donations, gifts from members of the congregation. None of the pieces matched, of course. But each was a gift from the heart, and therefore special.

But Sam didn't seem to notice the hole

in the upholstery. Instead, he continued to stare at Emilie. "How old is she?"

"Just a couple of months. Isn't she beautiful?"

The stove buzzer went off, interrupting whatever he might have said.

"Would you hold her while I check on the vegetables?"

Sam gave Emilie a cautious look. "Uh . . . she won't break, will she?"

Carla laughed. "No, she won't break. Babies are much tougher than they look. Just support her head and her back. Like this." She settled one hand under the baby's bottom and the other cradled her neck.

She handed Emilie to Sam, who took her gingerly, handing the bakery box to Carla as he did so. "Dessert," he said.

As Emilie snuggled into his arms, he looked down at her with a feeling akin to awe. Wonderingly, he watched as she curled a fist around his finger.

She cooed at him, her lips puckering into a tiny O. Her fingers closed around his silk tie, bringing it up to her mouth where she started to chew on it.

Gently, Carla disengaged Emilie's fingers. "I'm sorry. She likes the colors."

"It's all right." He looked down at his

now-crumpled tie. "I think I like it better this way."

She smiled at him approvingly. "You're doing fine," she said before disappearing into the kitchen.

Still wary, Sam held Emilie stiffly, breathing in the sweet scent of baby. He'd never been around children much. But the bundle in his arms convinced him he'd been missing something. "I could get to like you, little sweetheart."

The tiny hand tightened around his finger. He stroked her downy head; her tuft of white-blond hair reminded him of corn silk.

He'd been interviewed by dozens of reporters, had debated with opponents on television, and none of them intimidated him as much as the small bundle in his arms who stared up at him with dark-blue eyes.

"Look, I don't know what I'm supposed to do with you, but if I do anything wrong, just cry or something. Okay?"

A gurgle was the only response.

"I guess you don't talk much, do you? That's all right. I'll let you in on a secret. I've never really talked to a baby before."

Emilie continued to stare at him before erupting into a wail.

Sam panicked and dredged up everything he'd ever heard about babies. "Do you . . . uh . . . do you like to be walked?"

The crying momentarily halted as she looked up at him.

Taking that to be a "yes," he circled the room, all the while talking to Emilie.

"Maybe we should sit down for a while," he said and stopped.

The crying began again.

"Okay, okay. I get the message." They resumed their pacing. Sam kept up a steady stream of talk, weaving stories around a princess named Emilie, a fire-eating dragon, and a wicked duke who wanted to marry her.

". . . and then the prince charged through the palace gates, slew the dragon, and rescued Princess Emilie from the evil duke. They lived happily ever after."

A smile creased her face.

"Like that, do you?"

She rewarded him with another smile, followed by a series of hiccups. Each one shook her entire body.

"Hey, are you all right?"

Emilie found her fist, which she began to suck noisily.

"Should you be doing that?"

Ignoring him, she switched fists and continued sucking.

Sam kept walking and wondered how he'd managed to end up spending a Friday night baby-sitting. Not that he minded. In fact, he was enjoying himself. Emilie shifted slightly in his arms, and he automatically tightened his hold.

He looked down at her, surprised by the feelings of tenderness that assailed him. He smiled. Of course, he'd always been a sucker for blond hair and blue eyes. Lately, though, he'd been thinking of dark hair, silky dark hair.

"You're going to break a lot of hearts in a few years," he murmured.

Emilie rewarded him with another smile.

"A lot of hearts," he repeated. "Your daddy's going to have to beat the boys off with a stick."

A slight cough alerted him that he and Emilie were no longer alone. He looked up to find Carla smiling at him. Sam hadn't blushed since he was thirteen years old, but he was blushing now. He could feel the hot color flood his cheeks. How long had she been watching them?

"It's all right, Sam," Carla said. "There's nothing wrong with liking babies. Most people do."

"I . . . uh . . . I've never held a baby before." A smile slid past his embarrassment. "Guess it's pretty obvious, huh?"

"Never," she denied. "I'd say you're a real pro."

"Really?"

"Really."

A suspicious warmth spread over his shirt. "Uh-oh."

"What is it?"

He held Emilie out, at the same time trying to pull the shirt away from his chest. "I think she needs a diaper change."

He watched as Carla struggled not to laugh. A reluctant grin spread across his face. "I think I've just been christened."

"I think you're right. Give her to me and take off your shirt. I'll put it in the washer. It'll be done before you leave."

He handed the baby to Carla, surprised by the emptiness he felt without Emilie in his arms. A bit self-conscious, he unbuttoned his shirt and yanked it off, the wet material clinging to his skin.

Carla passed Emilie back to Sam and disappeared with his shirt. She came back carrying a pink terry robe. "I thought you might like this until your shirt's ready. I'm sorry I don't have anything bigger."

He gave Emilie back to Carla and took

the robe. He stuck his arms through the sleeves and tied the belt around him. The sleeves barely reached his elbows; the hem of the robe hit him at mid thigh.

"Go ahead and laugh," he said. "I know I look ridiculous."

A low laugh bubbled from her. After a minute, Sam joined her.

"You're a good sport. Not all men would take it this well." She grinned mischievously. "You look good in pink."

"I'll remember that the next time I buy a robe."

Their laughter mingled as they looked at each other. Sam put out a hand. "Carla, I —"

Emilie squirmed in her arms, interrupting what he wanted to say.

"Come on, Emilie," Carla crooned. "We're going to give you a dry bottom."

"May I watch?"

"Sure." She led the way to the bathroom, where she stripped Emilie of the wet diaper, washed and powdered her, and fastened the tapes of a disposable diaper.

To Sam's surprise, Emilie didn't cry during the proceedings. She giggled when Carla pressed a kiss to her tummy and kicked her chubby legs.

"You make it seem easy," he said, impressed with Carla's efficiency.

"It *is* easy." She gave him an impish smile. "You can do the next one."

"I think I'll pass next time." With a start, he realized what he'd just said. *Next time?* Would there be a next time? Spending an evening baby-sitting wasn't his usual idea of a good time, but then Carla Stevens wasn't the usual kind of woman.

Emilie yawned widely, drawing Sam's and Carla's attention.

Carla snapped the sleeper in place. "I'll just lay her down," she said, patting the baby on the back. "Then we can eat."

The meal of pot roast and vegetables was a far cry from the elegant dinner they'd shared two nights ago. And far more enjoyable, Sam admitted silently. No snowy linen or fine china adorned the table, only place mats, stoneware dishes, and a glass holding a bouquet of wildflowers.

Perhaps it was the setting. Carla's homey kitchen had its own brand of charm, wrapping itself around him, inviting him to relax. It was working, Sam recognized, as he helped himself to another slice of roast and helping of vegetables.

He looked up to find Carla smiling. "I don't usually eat this much. After a while, restaurant food all starts to taste the same. A home-cooked meal is a real treat."

"Don't apologize. I'm glad you like it."

"You ought to open your own restaurant. I'd be your first and best customer."

"I have a job," she said quietly.

"I know." Feeling like he'd blundered, he searched for something to say and remembered the cheesecake he'd brought.

"Shall we have dessert?"

He supposed the cheesecake was good, but he barely tasted it. He was too busy staring at Carla. She'd worn her hair loose. It tumbled around her face in a mass of dark curls. Sooty lashes framed eyes as blue as Emilie's.

As he'd done two nights ago, he took her hand, liking the feel of it nestled in his. Her nails were free of polish, her fingers bare of rings. This time, she didn't pull her hand away. Encouraged, he continued to hold it until Carla gently removed it from his hand.

"If you'd like to wait in the living room, you could turn on the TV. I'll just be a few minutes cleaning up."

She started to stack dishes.

"Let me help. Please," he added when he saw the uncertainty on her face.

"You don't have to."

"I know. But I want to," he said, surprised to find the words were true. He did want to help. He wanted to spend time with her, even if it meant washing dishes. Besides, he had a feeling that washing dishes would be enjoyable with Carla.

They worked side by side in companionable silence. They quickly developed a rhythm of Carla washing the dishes and then handing them to Sam, who dried them.

Bubbles danced through the air as she squirted more detergent into the water. Some settled in her hair, glistening like diamonds against sable. Another landed on the tip of her nose. Without thinking, Sam reached up to wipe the bubble away. His hand collided with hers.

She dropped her hand and reached for a towel, dabbing it at her face.

"You should always wear bubbles." His fingers sifted through her hair. "Here." He dropped his hand to touch her nose. "And here."

"Maybe I could start a trend."

"It'd never catch on. Any woman can wear diamonds. Only a few can wear bubbles."

"Thank you," she said softly. "That's the nicest compliment I've ever received."

"Then you've been seeing the wrong men."

She turned away and began gathering up the remaining dishes.

Sam took them from her and stacked them on the counter. "I'm sorry. Did I embarrass you?"

"No . . . that is, I don't date all that much. I don't have time."

"Maybe it's time for a change." Gently, so very gently, he fitted his lips to hers. She tasted sweet — incredibly sweet.

When he raised his head, he was shaken. "Don't ask me to apologize for that."

"I'm not going to. I enjoyed it."

Her honesty startled him almost as much as did the kiss. She was as guileless as a child, with her huge eyes gazing straight into his heart. He drew her to him, his hands resting at her waist.

He forgot that he was wearing a pink terry robe several sizes too small for him. He forgot that she was a minister, a world away from his own. He forgot everything . . . everything but the woman in his arms.

He didn't try to kiss her again. He was content to hold her, to feel her heart beat a rapid tatoo against his chest. Words were unnecessary, which was good, because he couldn't think of a thing to say.

A wail pierced the silence, shattering the mood.

Gently, Carla withdrew from his embrace. "I'd better check on Emilie."

Sam drew in a deep breath, not sure whether he was sorry or relieved by the interruption. Probably a little of both. What was he doing here anyway? He had no business becoming involved with Carla Stevens.

A few minutes later, she reappeared holding the baby who was sucking on a bottle. Carla then lifted Emilie to her shoulder and gently patted the tiny back.

The ensuing burp caused Sam to grin and snapped the tension between them. "Sounds like Emilie's feeling good."

"I think you're right."

He reached out to brush a finger across Emilie's cheek. It was as soft as it looked. He wondered what Carla's skin would feel like. Would it be baby-soft also? Somehow, he knew the answer already.

It would.

As soft as her heart. The thought surprised him. He wasn't given to poetic turns of phrases. But, then, Carla had him doing a lot of things he wasn't accustomed to. Things like holding a baby. Things like clearing a table and washing dishes. Things like kissing a lady minister.

Things like wanting to kiss her again.

"I . . . uh, I'd better go."

Did she look disappointed? He hoped so. He knew *he* was. But right now, he needed time away, time to put his thoughts — his feelings — into perspective. He couldn't do that when he was near Carla.

"May I call you?" he asked.

A smile chased away the disappointment — if it were disappointment — from her face. "Of course. Would you take Emilie for a minute? I'll get your shirt."

Chagrined, Sam looked down at the pink robe. He'd forgotten that he still wore it.

Emilie stared up at him. Was that reproach in her eyes? Of course not. He was imagining things. But her eyes continued to hold him with a nonblinking gaze. "Okay. I'm a coward. I admit it."

Emilie's brow puckered into a tiny frown.

"Carla's special," he said. "I don't want to hurt her."

Carla returned just then. Had she heard?

"It's still warm from the dryer," she said as she handed the shirt to him and took Emilie.

He shrugged off the robe and slipped into the shirt, not caring how he buttoned it. Right now all he wanted was to get out of here.

Much as he'd done with Emilie earlier,

he brushed a finger across Carla's cheek, not trusting himself to kiss her again. He'd been right. Her skin was as soft as Emilie's.

Chapter Three

Pulling aside the drapes, Carla watched as he drove away.

Sam Hastings was a funny kind of man. He was brusque and blunt one moment, gentle and warm the next. He was also way out of her league.

Settling into a rocking chair, she rocked Emilie, the steady motion soothing her mixed-up emotions. Looking into the baby's oh-so-blue eyes, Carla wondered what Emilie thought of Sam. Even while she was berating herself for the silliness of the question, Carla couldn't help noticing that Emilie smiled.

"You liked him too, didn't you?"

The baby cooed.

"I'm not surprised," Carla said. "He's the kind of man who appeals to women of all ages — young and old."

Emilie cooed again, a sound Carla took for agreement. She picked the baby up and held her against her. Emilie snuggled in the hollow of Carla's shoulder, making the soft baby sounds that swaddled her heart with pangs of longing.

"Sam's right. You're going to break a lot of hearts in a few years."

When Emilie's parents returned, Carla bundled the baby into her blanket and pressed a kiss to her head. She waved good-bye and tried not to feel lonely as the young family departed amid a flurry of thank-yous.

Her arms felt empty without the sweet weight of a baby filling them, and she allowed herself a rare moment of self-pity. She yearned for her own children, her own family. She spent most of her time surrounded by people, yet she was frequently lonely. At that moment, she remembered Sam's comments about her personal life.

He was wrong.

Her life was full. She didn't have time for the emptiness he'd accused her of trying to fill. But she couldn't stop the wayward thoughts as she finished cleaning up the kitchen.

Chances were good she wouldn't be hearing from him again. After that one breathtaking kiss, he'd beat a hasty exit. It didn't take too much reasoning to figure out why.

He'd been disappointed. She'd known all along that Sam was too sophisticated to be attracted to a woman like her. But she couldn't help the tiny cloud of disappointment that settled over her spirits.

He'd said he'd call. But that was probably an exit line. Well, that was all right with her. She didn't need a man complicating her life. She had enough on her plate, what with meeting the needs of the members of her congregation, raising funds for the community home, and keeping up with her other volunteer work.

No, she didn't need a man in her life right now. But sometimes . . . sometimes she wished there were someone special. Someone to share the good times with as well as the bad. Someone to chase away the loneliness. Someone to . . . love.

When the phone shrilled, Carla picked it up on the first ring, eager to escape her thoughts.

"Reverend Stevens? It's Ethan Sandberg. Maude took a bad fall. She's at the hospital now and asking for you. I know it's late, but could you come?"

"I'll be there in ten minutes," Carla promised.

Maude and Ethan Sandberg were two of Carla's favorite people. Despite their years, they managed to run rings around most people half their age. But a fall at eighty was serious.

Carla drove quickly, grateful the traffic was light at this time of night. She made it to the hospital in eight minutes and walked straight to the admitting desk. The receptionist directed her to the third floor, where she found Ethan pacing.

"Thank you for coming, Reverend Stevens," he said, pressing her hand between his gnarled ones.

"I'm glad you called me. How is she?"

"I don't know. The doctor's with her now. I'm afraid she broke her hip." His voice cracked. "What if . . . what if . . . ?" He sniffled loudly and then cleared his throat. "Maude and I have been together the best part of sixty years."

"She's going to be all right," Carla said, praying her words were true. She led him to a mustard-colored couch. "Would you like some coffee?"

Ethan managed a smile. "Please."

"I'll be right back." She walked down a corridor until she found a coffee machine and fed quarters into it. Balancing two Styrofoam cups, she rejoined Ethan and handed him one.

She took a sip and grimaced. The coffee, as black as sludge and twice as thick, burned its way down her throat. She made herself take another sip, knowing she'd need the jolt of caffeine before the night was over.

"I don't want you worrying," she said, setting the cup aside. "Maude's strong. She's not going to let a fall keep her down for long."

Ethan's face brightened. "You're right. Maude's a trouper. Did I tell you about the time she. . . ."

Carla listened to a story she'd heard a dozen times before, but she didn't mind. She held Ethan's hand, squeezing it when his voice wavered, pretending not to notice when his eyes filled with tears.

When the doctor appeared, they both stood.

"Mr. Sandberg, I'm Dr. Franckum. Your wife broke her hip during the fall. I've set it. She's still under sedation right now and probably will stay that way for the next few hours."

Ethan's hand tightened around Carla's. "Is she . . . is she going to be all right?"

The doctor gestured toward the couch. "Why don't we sit down?"

Carla slipped an arm around Ethan's shoulders and helped him back to the couch. The torn vinyl crackled as they sat down. He tried to speak, couldn't, and turned to Carla, his face mirroring all he couldn't say.

"I'm Reverend Stevens, Doctor," she said quietly. "I'm also a friend of Ethan and Maude's."

"I'm glad you're here." The doctor shifted his attention back to Ethan. "Mr. Sandberg, your wife is going to be all right." He paused. "Eventually. But she's going to need a lot of care, even when she comes out of the hospital."

"That's no problem," Ethan said quickly. "I'll take care of her. Just like she'd do for me."

Dr. Franckum and Carla exchanged looks. "She may need more care than you can give her," he said gently and stood. "Look, we don't need to make any decision right away. It'll be a while before your wife will be able to leave here. Why don't you go home and get some sleep? You can see her in the morning."

Ethan struggled to his feet. "Thank you, Doctor. But I'm not leaving. Maude might need me. We haven't spent a night apart in sixty years. I don't intend on starting now."

The doctor smiled slightly. "I thought you might feel that way. I'll arrange for a bed for you in her room." He signaled a nurse. "Reverend Stevens, may I talk with you for a minute?"

Carla patted Ethan's shoulder. "I'll be right back."

She walked with Dr. Franckum down the hallway until they were out of earshot. "Is Maude's condition more serious than you said?"

"Mrs. Sandberg sustained a bad fracture to her hip. At her age and with her bones as brittle as they are, she might well never recover completely. Someone needs to prepare her husband that she might never be able to come home."

Tears stung her eyes, but she blinked them away. "I think it'd kill Ethan to be separated from Maude."

"Do they have any other family?"

"They lost their only son a few years ago. But they have friends — lots of friends."

"I'm glad. They're going to need them." The doctor pushed his glasses back on his nose and sighed. "I've been doing this for twelve years. It never gets any easier."

Carla accompanied Ethan to Maude's room. The slight, pale figure in the bed in no way resembled the active, bright-eyed woman Carla knew, and she hesitated in the doorway.

But not Ethan.

He crossed the room to stand beside his wife's bed. Gently, he lifted her hand and pressed it to his cheek. "It's going to be all right, Maudie," he said, tears streaming down his face. "It's going to be all right." He sat by her bed and held her hand, refusing to lie down on the other bed the doctor had provided.

Carla stayed with Ethan until morning. She nibbled on a candy bar and finished the coffee. It was cold now and bitter enough to shock her taste buds.

She returned home, exhausted, worried, and hungry. But overriding everything else was the warm feeling that washed over her as she remembered the love she'd witnessed between Ethan and Maude.

It was a love that had lasted sixty years. A love to last a lifetime. The kind of love she wanted for herself.

Unbidden, her mind conjured up a picture of Sam holding Emilie and talking nonsense to her, his strong hands gentle as he cradled her against him.

Impatiently, Carla brushed the image aside. Obviously, she was more tired than she'd thought.

At his office, Sam reflected on his feelings for Carla. She intrigued him; she provoked him; she scared him more than a little.

He wasn't sure of anything except that he had to see her again. After the way he'd bolted from her house two nights ago, he wouldn't be at all surprised if she didn't want to see him again. He didn't blame her; he'd acted like a jerk.

Idly, he doodled her name on a piece of paper.

"I don't know where your mind is, Sam, but it's obviously not on strategy."

"What . . . oh, sorry." Guiltily, Sam looked up to find Jerry tapping his fingers impatiently against the desk. "What were you saying?"

"I was saying that we need to push your image as a man of the people. Your stint in the Marines helps, but you need something more. Right now, you've got the upper hand, but you're seen as a little aloof, removed from the average person. Your family background doesn't help any either. People are suspicious of what they see as the rich and privileged."

Sam couldn't help the groan of frustration that escaped his lips. His family background, his looks, his friends, everything about him seemed to be grist for the media, everything except what he believed, what he stood for.

"What do you suggest I do? Disown my parents and pretend I'm not their son? I didn't choose to be born to wealthy parents, but I'm not going to spend my life apologizing for it." He took a deep breath. "Does anyone know that I worked for everything I have? Does anyone *care?*"

Jerry held up a hand. "Don't get on your high horse with me, Sam. I know you started the business on your own. I also know you didn't take a cent from your parents."

"Then what's the problem?"

"You just need to project yourself more as someone the common man can relate to."

"Jerry, I appreciate what you're doing for me, but I'm the one running for election. Not my family. Not my background. If that's not good enough for the people, then I won't get elected. It's as simple as that."

Jerry let loose with a low string of words that Sam didn't bother to listen to. "All right," Jerry said at last. "What about this lady minister you're seeing? We might be able to use that."

"Carla? She's a friend, nothing more." Was that the truth? Or did he simply want it to be the truth?

"What about her involvement in the

homeless issue? That's a hot item. Isn't she one of the group moving to have a community home built? We'll play that up, make it look like you —"

"Leave it alone, Jerry. Reverend Stevens wouldn't take kindly to having the project being used as a publicity gimmick." Sam let a thread of steel run through his voice. "Neither would I."

"Okay, okay." Jerry gave in with a resigned sigh. "Would it be all right if I arranged for you to attend a Rotary meeting next Tuesday? Maybe give a short speech?"

Sam grinned at the uncharacteristic humility in Jerry's voice. "Sure."

"Great." Jerry gathered up his papers into a messy pile, stuffed them into his briefcase, and slapped Sam on the back. "We're going to win this thing, buddy. Just wait and see. In the meantime, trust me. I know what I'm doing." He gave Sam one last look. "Wear something casual."

Sam walked Jerry to the door and then closed it behind him.

He turned his attention back to his desk, which held bids on two new projects. If he expected to have a business, he had to start spending more time working at it. The campaign had eaten up more time than he'd believed possible.

He punched the intercom. "Sarah, hold my calls for the next two hours."

At noon, Sam looked at the next folder awaiting his attention. He rotated his shoulders in an effort to relieve the tension that had knotted itself in a ball.

One more, he promised himself. And that was it. He'd already buzzed Sarah to ask her to order a corned beef on rye from the local deli. It'd been delivered over an hour ago, the wrapper and crumbs still littering his desk.

Jerry should see him now, Sam reflected. Wolfing down a sandwich at his desk should qualify him as one of the working stiffs of the world.

But Jerry thought in terms of publicity stunts, gimmicks, and catchy phrases. Not for the first time, Sam questioned the wisdom of having asked Jerry to be his campaign manager. He was too flashy, too slick for Sam's taste, but his father had recommended Jerry. Sam had reluctantly agreed, more to breach the gap between himself and his father than for anything else.

Sam frowned, recognizing what was really bothering him. His relationship with his father, never good, had improved dramatically since Sam had decided to run for

City Council. His father approved of what he viewed as Sam's foray into the political world. He'd brushed aside Sam's assertion that he was running for City Council to give something back to the city and its people.

Already his father was trying to bestow favors, favors Sam knew he'd be expected to repay by awarding city contracts to his father's friends and business associates. He'd known what politics was like when he decided to run for his office; he just hadn't expected the pressure to be applied so soon and by his own father.

Once more, Sam studied the demographic research Jerry had laid out. Jerry knew his stuff, there was no getting around it. He was just a tad overeager.

Sam looked at the phone, a guilty twinge tugging at his conscience. He'd promised Carla he'd call. But he hadn't. It wasn't from a lack of desire to see her again. On the contrary, he wanted to see her again — very much.

He turned his attention back to the file and finished a preliminary sketch for a building design. A smile of satisfaction rested briefly on his lips.

He buzzed Sarah's office. "Done."

"Do you want messages?"

He thought about it. The last thing he wanted to do was to spend the rest of the day returning calls. Right now, he needed to work off some of the pent-up energy that resulted from confining himself to a desk all morning.

"No. Unless there's something urgent, save 'em for tomorrow."

Letting himself out the backdoor of his office, he punched the number of the ground floor of his private elevator. Five minutes later, he was in his truck, heading out of the parking garage.

He drove quickly, not knowing where he was heading until he found himself outside the apartments Carla had taken him to last week. He hadn't been able to shake the picture of the dilapidated apartments from his mind.

If he were elected, cleaning up this place and others like it was going to be one of his first orders of business. He walked inside the front door, noticing, as he'd done last week, the lack of security. Anyone could walk in, tenant or not. Even George and his cronies were absent, probably driven inside by the cold.

It was only slightly warmer in the lobby, and he huddled deeper into his coat. He took his time climbing the stairs and walking down the hallways, trying to understand how people forced to live here must feel.

The sounds of misery rumbled through the building. From one apartment, a baby cried, the long, steady wails tugging at Sam's heart. Curses and shrieks penetrated the walls of another. Something small and dark scuttled across his foot and into a hole in the wall.

The ripe smell of garbage, spoiled food, and mildew assailed his nostrils. But underlying the foul odors was a subtler, though no less potent, smell, one soap and water wouldn't wash away. The smell of despair. Of dying hopes, forgotten dreams, shattered faith.

Carla had tried to tell him this when she'd brought him here, but he'd been too appalled by the physical conditions to understand what she'd meant. Now he was beginning to understand.

The question was, what was he going to do about it?

He knocked at Mona Freeman's apartment but found no one home. He exited the building quickly, ashamed of the relief he felt upon walking outside. He inhaled deeply. Even the polluted air tasted fresh compared to the stench inside.

He unlocked his car, turned on the ignition, and eased the car into the snarl of late-afternoon traffic. This time, he knew where he was going.

Chapter Four

"I didn't expect to see you today," Carla said.

He followed her inside. He didn't have any trouble reading between the lines. She hadn't expected to see him again. After the way he'd left two nights ago, he didn't blame her.

"I should have called first."

"No. I'm glad you came." She gestured toward the couch. "Sit down."

She perched on the arm of a chair and looked at him expectantly.

"I visited the Royal Arms today."

Her eyes widened, but she said nothing.

"I tried what you said — looking with my heart instead of my eyes."

"What did you see?"

"Despair. People who'd given up on their dreams." He paused, searching for the right words with which to apologize. The compassion in her eyes convinced him he didn't need fancy words; he only needed to say what was in his heart. "I'm sorry. You must have thought I was a real jerk that first day, especially when I offered to write you a check."

She shook her head. "I thought you were someone who cared but didn't understand."

"And now?"

"I think you're beginning to realize that money isn't the whole answer."

For the first time, he noticed the shadows beneath her eyes. They gave her a bruised look that tugged at his sympathy. He'd come here, trying to absolve his guilt, and had been oblivious to anyone's distress but his own. "Didn't you sleep well?"

"I spent the last two nights at the hospital with a friend."

He listened while she sketched in the details of Maude and Ethan Sandberg. Her voice quavered several times, telling him more clearly than words how deeply she cared about the elderly couple.

"Maude and Ethan are so much in love. If something happens to one, it happens to the other."

He saw her throat move as she swallowed her worry.

"I don't even want to think what would happen if Maude has to go to a nursing home. They've been married over sixty years and still act like newlyweds."

"Even after all those years," he murmured. How many marriages lasted five years, much less sixty?

"It's *because* of all those years. Maude's told me more than once that love grows with the years. She and Ethan are proof of that."

Sam knew of too many marriages where the love had stopped growing and had turned into some ugly and painful, but he was warmed by the picture she drew of Ethan and Maude Sandberg. In his estimation, though, theirs was the exception rather than the rule.

Thoughts of his parents' marriage hardened his face. His mother, with her endless charity and social functions, and his father, one of the power brokers of the city, shared nothing in common but a mutual desire to keep up appearances. Sam learned a long time ago that he was not a son to either but a pawn to be used against each other.

But he didn't share those thoughts with Carla. He didn't want to see the compassion in her eyes if he were to tell her the truth about his so-called privileged childhood.

"You almost make me believe in happily-ever-afters," he murmured, more to himself than her.

"You mean you don't?"

"Not usually. I'm too much of a realist.

But listening to you, I'm inclined to revise my views."

"I hope so, Sam," she said earnestly. "Believing in the good things of life is important. It's what keeps us going during the bad times."

Listening to her, he was reminded again of how far apart their worlds were. Hers was full of hope, light, and finding the good wherever she looked; his was bottom lines, campaign strategies, and underbidding his competitors.

Could two such worlds harmonize? The question startled him. Since when had he started thinking in those terms? He didn't bother to puzzle over the answers. He only knew he wanted to spend time with this woman who wove love into everything she touched. Perhaps some of her magic would rub off on him.

"May I see you tonight?" he asked.

She shook her head. "I'm sorry," she said, sounding like she really meant it. "I promised to stop by the hospital and spell Ethan for a couple of hours. He needs to stop by their house and pick up a few things for himself and Maude, but he doesn't want to leave her alone."

"What about the nurses? Won't they be around?"

"It's not the same. Ethan won't leave her with only strangers to care for her."

"And you're filling in the gap?"

"I want to. I'd have gone to the hospital even if Ethan hadn't asked me."

And she would have, he knew. Carla Stevens seemed to have an endless supply of energy. And love.

"I'll drive you."

She smiled. "That's nice of you to offer, but I don't know how long I'll be there."

"The county hospital's in a rough section of town. I don't want you coming home late at night."

"Sam, I'm a big girl," she said gently. "I've been taking care of myself for a long time now."

"I know, but I want to help. Let me take you. When you're done, call me and I'll pick you up."

He didn't know how much it meant to him until she nodded.

"All right. I'd appreciate it."

"What time do you want to leave?" he asked.

"Ethan asked that I come around seven. Is that all right with you?"

Sam nodded, relieved she was letting him do this for her.

When he picked her up at a quarter of

seven, he motioned to a sack on the seat.
"I picked up some dinner for you."

Carla opened it up, finding a variety
of Mexican food from a local fast-food
restaurant. "It smells wonderful." She un-
wrapped a taco and bit into it. "And tastes
even better."

Sam smiled at her obvious enjoyment of
the simple food. With any other woman,
he'd never have considered buying her
tacos and burritos for dinner. But Carla
acted as though he'd taken her to a five-
star restaurant.

She offered him a taco, but he refused.
"I had dinner an hour ago."

He frowned, remembering their dinner
of a few nights ago. She'd been uncomfortable at the extravagance. She'd appreciated
the simple fast-food meal far more.

"How did you know this is just what I
needed?" she asked.

"I'm beginning to know you. I figured
you'd be too busy to fix yourself something
to eat."

"You figured right." She dug further into
the bag and produced a couple of packets
of hot sauce. Spreading a napkin over her
lap, she squirted them onto the burrito. "I
love Mexican food. The hotter, the better."

They arrived at the hospital just as she

finished the last of the food. She dabbed at her lips with the napkin. "Thank you."

"Mind if I come in?" he asked, pulling the car into a parking space. "I'd like to meet Ethan. And Maude, if she's up to having visitors. You've told me so much about them, I feel like I know them already."

She looked pleased at his request. "I'd like that."

County Hospital showed its age. Like a proud old lady who had once stood straight and tall, she was now bent with the years and ravages of time. The once-white limestone was grayed, the wood trim in need of painting, the grounds unkempt.

The hospital received part of its funding from the city, but it obviously wasn't enough, Sam thought, as he followed Carla to the elevators. The vinyl sofa and chairs in the lobby area were cracked, the walls dingy, the linoleum yellowed.

Once again, he was reminded of how much needed to be done. If he were elected, he'd have his work cut out for him. The city fathers didn't like spending money unnecessarily. They didn't like spending money, period.

They found Ethan pacing impatiently up and down the corridor. "The doctor has some kind of specialist in there with her," he said, jerking his thumb to Maude's room. "Won't let me in. Me — her husband!" His voice rose in indignation.

Carla slipped an arm around his shoulder, leading him to the sofa where she gently pushed him down. "They just want to examine her."

"I know. But I want to be with her. She's probably scared, asking for me." Ethan looked up and saw Sam. "Who's this? Your young man?"

"This is Sam Hastings," Carla said. "A friend."

Ethan studied Sam in an unhurried way before sticking out his hand. "Looks all right. He might do. Pleased to meet you."

Sam shook hands and noticed two things. First, the soft color that smudged Carla's cheeks. Second, Ethan's protective attitude toward her.

He wasn't surprised at the feelings Carla engendered in the older man. Sam felt the same way himself. Well, not quite the same way.

"How's Maude doing?" Carla asked.

Ethan slumped back onto the sofa. "All right, I guess. She was groggy this morning from the pain medication they've got her on."

"That's to be expected," Sam said.

"I know," Ethan said. "I'm hoping she'll feel better tonight."

Carla touched his shoulder. "Ethan, if you want to go home and get those things now, I'll stay with Maude until you get back."

"I'd appreciate it," Ethan said. "Will your young man be keeping you company?"

"No," Carla said quickly. "He was just dropping me off. He'll be back later to pick me up."

"I'd like to stay," Sam said. "If it's all right."

Carla looked from Sam to Ethan and back to Sam again. "I guess that'd be all right."

Ethan brightened visibly. "It'd do Maude good to see you two young people together. It'll remind her of the days when we were courting."

"But Sam and I aren't . . . that is, we don't . . . I mean —" Carla broke off the jumbled stream of words and sent a warning glance at Sam.

"What do you mean?" Sam asked, mischief lighting his brown eyes with golden sparks.

"We're just friends," Carla said at last, glaring at him.

She watched as Ethan and Sam exchanged man-to-man looks that effectively excluded her.

"Well, be that as it may," Ethan said, "it'd still do Maude a world of good to see you two together. She needs something to keep her mind occupied. You know, she's been wanting to see you get hitched for a long time, Reverend. Many's a time she's said to me, 'Reverend Stevens needs a man and babes of her own to care for.'"

Carla could feel the blush creep from the base of her neck up her face. She saw Sam trying to stifle a grin. He wasn't being very successful at it, judging from the way his mouth was twitching.

"You'd better go while you can," she said to Ethan. "We'll take care of things here."

Ethan thanked them both and headed to the elevators, leaving Carla and Sam alone.

"I apologize for Ethan," she said as she and Sam made themselves comfortable on the couch.

"What for?"

She gave him an exasperated look. "For what he said. He's obviously under a lot of strain and was rambling. People tend to do that when they're upset or worried."

"Ethan has every cause to be worried,

but I don't think he was rambling. I think he showed a lot of insight."

Carla was saved from responding to that by the appearance of the doctor.

"Reverend Stevens, it's nice to see you again." Dr. Franckum looked about. "Did Mr. Sandberg go home?"

"He wanted to pick up a few things for himself and Maude. How is she?"

"Much better than I ever believed possible," the doctor said, scratching his head. "By all rights, she ought to be feeling pretty low, but she's already started to give me a hard time about letting her out of here." He gave an admiring shake of his head. "She's remarkable."

"May we see her?" Carla asked.

"For a little while. She still tires easily, but she could use the company. That woman can talk like no one I've ever met. When she found out I was single, she told me to find a nice young woman and settle down."

Carla and Sam chuckled.

"I'll see you later," the doctor said, already bent over his clipboard and walking away.

Carla knocked at the door and received an impatient, "Come in."

She opened it and found Maude

propped up in bed. She seemed in good spirits. "Reverend Stevens, you're spoiling me with your visits." She fixed her gaze on Sam. "Who's your friend?"

Carla made the introductions, blushing again at Maude's open scrutiny of Sam.

"Glad to meet you, Mrs. Sandberg," Sam said, taking the hand she offered.

"Sit down, sit down," Maude ordered. "Make yourselves comfortable and stay a while. Reverend Stevens, you've been an angel to sit with Ethan and me the last two nights, but we don't expect you to babysit us each night."

"I like being here, Maude. You know that."

"I know," the older woman said. "I also know you need to get out with young people more, not spend your evenings cooped up with two old people like us."

Before Carla could object, Maude turned her attention to Sam. "Tell me about yourself, young man."

Sam sent a look of appeal to Carla which she ignored. She was going to enjoy this. Maude could get a turnip to talk, as she was proud of boasting.

"I'm thirty-two, of sound mind and body, and have all my own teeth."

Maude chuckled. "Can you dance?"

"Yes, ma'am. And meaning no disrespect, but if you were up and about, I'd ask you to go dancing with me, husband or not."

"Full of vinegar. Just like Ethan was at your age." Maude winked broadly at Carla. "He still is."

Carla decided it was time to intervene. "Sam and I are just friends. He's interested in the community home project."

Maude leveled a disappointed look at Sam. "Well, I can't fault you for giving a hand with a worthy cause, but if that's all you want with our Carla here, then you're not the man I took you for."

"With all due respect, ma'am, I am interested in the project. I want to see that home built just as much as Carla does. But that's not the only thing I want."

"And what would the other be?"

"I want to date your minister." He put out his hands in a gesture of appeal. "Care to put in a good word for me?"

Maude grinned. "I like him, Reverend. Dang if I don't. He's a right 'un. Don't let him get away."

Carla noticed Sam's shoulders shaking. He was enjoying this altogether too much. "Maude, I appreciate your interest, but —"

"Shush, girl. I want to hear more about your young man." She gave Sam a keen look. "Haven't I seen your picture some-where?"

"Sam's running for City Council," Carla said. "You've probably seen him on TV and in the papers."

Maude snapped her fingers. "That's it. You planning on doing something for the city or just sitting on your duff like those good-for-nothings we've got in there now? Bunch of pantywaists, if you ask me."

Carla started to protest when Sam cut in. "I'm planning on doing everything I can to make this a city to be proud of."

"See that you do. Or you'll answer to me."

"Yes, ma'am," he answered meekly.

Maude jabbed him in the chest with a bony finger. "There's a church potluck on Saturday. Won't be as good as usual be-cause I won't be there to bring my fried chicken. But the rest of the ladies cook passable good. I want you to bring the Reverend. She doesn't get out enough, not near enough. It would do her good to be squired around with a handsome young man like yourself."

"I'd be glad to oblige, ma'am."

"Now just a minute," Carla said. "Don't I get anything to say about this?"

"No," Sam and Maude said in unison.

Chuckling, Maude patted Sam's hand. "You're a right 'un, all right. Just like my Ethan."

Carla started to give Sam a piece of her mind when she saw Maude's face. Laugh lines had replaced the lines of pain and worry that had been there earlier. For that alone, she could forgive Sam anything.

Well, almost anything, she amended as she watched the way he and Maude put their heads together, discussing something in low voices. Just what were they cooking up?

Sam and Carla stayed until Ethan returned. By then, Sam and Maude were trading stories and lies like old friends. Carla had taken a back seat, content to listen and put in an occasional word.

Ethan crossed the room to kiss Maude. "Look at you. You're prettier than you were when I first laid eyes on you at the cotillion at the old courthouse."

Maude blushed, Ethan crowed, and Carla felt tears rush to her eyes. Maude and Ethan seemed to have that effect on her. She dug in her purse for a tissue and dabbed at her eyes, hoping no one would notice. When she looked up, she found Sam's gaze on her.

"Something in my eye," she murmured.

"Something like how Maude and Ethan make you feel," he said softly. "Don't be ashamed of your feelings, Carla." He touched her cheek, tracing the trail a tear had left. "Or your tears."

"I'm not ashamed. Just embarrassed."

"Not on my account, I hope."

She darted a glance back at Ethan and Maude. They were so wrapped up in each other that they weren't paying any attention to her and Sam.

"Maybe we should go," she whispered.

He nodded. "I'm beginning to feel a little superfluous."

They made their good-byes with promises to come again.

"Reverend, you bring Sam back with you when you come again, you hear?" Maude said. "He's a corker. And Sam, come by anytime. You're good for an old woman."

"I'd be happy to visit you, Maude," he said, stooping to drop a kiss on her forehead. "But I don't see any old women around."

Her laughter followed them out the door.

In the hallway, Carla turned on him. "Why did you encourage Maude to think we're . . . we're . . ."

"We're what?"

"Seeing each other."

"Aren't we?"

"No. At least, not that way."

"Then what way are we seeing each other?"

"The way . . . the way friends see each other."

"Oh. Does that mean you're taking back the invitation to the church potluck dinner?"

"Yes — I mean no. Maude would never forgive me if I told her you didn't come."

"Is that the only reason you want me to come?" he asked, reaching around her to push the elevator button. "Because of Maude?"

"Yes." The lie tasted sour upon her lips. "No, it's not." She took a deep breath. "I want you to come."

"Why?"

"Because of me."

"Was that so hard?" he asked gently.

"Yes."

"Then let me make it easier." He lowered his head to kiss her right there in the elevator.

The elevator reached the ground floor. The door opened. And Sam continued to kiss her. When he raised his head, a smattering of applause greeted them.

"You see?" he asked. "I've got supporters."

"What you've got is a lot of nerve." But the smile she shot him took any sting from the words.

On the drive home, Carla thought about his question.

The kiss didn't make things any easier. If anything, it made them more difficult, and she almost told him not to come to the potluck after all. But something stopped her.

Something like the way he looked at her . . . as if she were the most beautiful woman in the world.

Under the porch light, he drew her to him once more, but this time she pulled away from the hands that gently held her. She couldn't chance another kiss. Not when her feelings were in such turmoil. "It's getting late."

"What time is the potluck?"

"What? Oh . . . seven. We're not real punctual about starting on time."

"One more question. Just what exactly is potluck?"

"You've never been to a potluck dinner before?"

He shook his head. " 'Fraid not."

"Everybody brings something to share."

"A bottle of wine?"

"The church provides the drink. We're

having lemonade." She laughed at his expression. "You don't have to bring anything. I'll bring something for both of us."

She expected him to share her smile, but his expression sobered as he looked at her, and once more he surprised her.

"I'll be bringing the most beautiful woman there." He touched his lips to hers and then left.

Only when she heard the engine of his car roar to life did she realize she was still standing on the porch.

Chapter Five

By Saturday morning, Carla was congratulating herself on inviting Sam to the potluck. She couldn't have come up with anything better to point out the differences between them if she'd tried. Sam was pâté and champagne; she was meat loaf and root beer. He'd take one look at the church social and run as fast as he could. She pushed away the stab of disappointment and told herself it was for the best.

She spent the morning boiling potatoes for German potato salad, her contribution to the potluck. By afternoon, she was over at the church, helping set up the long folding tables used for church dinners.

"You shouldn't be doing that," Mr. Porter, who worked as the part-time janitor, said. "A little thing like you."

She hefted her side of the table and propped open the legs. "I can handle it if you can."

He grinned. "Guess you can at that."

They worked together setting up a dozen more tables.

"Heard you were seeing a young man," Mr. Porter said, elaborately casual.

Carla bit back a sigh. News traveled fast on the church's grapevine. No doubt it started with Ethan Sandberg and had been embellished along the way. She wouldn't be surprised if the church gossip had her married and expecting her first child by now.

"I see lots of people."

He gave her a reproachful look. "No need to get uppity. You know we're just looking out for you, Reverend Stevens. A woman alone needs someone to look out for her. It don't hurt a man to know a lady's got people who care about her. Keeps him on his toes."

A smile slipped past her annoyance. She couldn't mistake the interest in his eyes for anything but genuine concern. "I know. I'm sorry."

"That's all right. A woman in love is entitled to be a trifle touchy."

"But I'm not —" She stopped at his knowing smile.

When the church ladies arrived to decorate and set the tables with paper plates and plastic utensils, Carla had heard a dozen different versions of how she'd met "her young man," none of which came anywhere close to the truth. Questions ranged from what his intentions were to how soon they were getting married.

She managed to hold on to her sense of humor throughout the gentle-but-thorough inquisition, but she was feeling sorely tried by the time she reached home.

"Sam Hastings, this is all your fault."

She poked a finger at the newspaper, which featured a picture of Sam on the first page. The paper was a couple of days old, but she'd saved it, telling herself she hadn't had a chance to finish reading it. She conveniently dismissed the fact that she rarely read the paper completely through.

She spent the next hour showering and washing her hair. When Sam arrived to pick her up a few minutes before seven, she was dragging a comb through her still-damp hair.

"Not every woman looks gorgeous with wet hair," he said, twirling an errant curl around his finger.

Her earlier indignation faded at the warmth in his eyes. She couldn't stay angry at this man. Not for long, anyway.

"I hope you're ready for the twentieth-century version of the Inquisition."

He cocked an eyebrow. "Care to explain that?"

"I think I'll let you find out for yourself."

"You're a hard-hearted woman, Carla Stevens," he said, helping her with her jacket.

"And you're not getting anything more out of me," she said, laughing up at him.

She was still chuckling as she retrieved her potato salad from the refrigerator. "Ready."

The church grounds had been transformed for the evening with miniature lights strung from trees and lampposts.

After introducing Sam to a few people, Carla took her potato salad to the kitchen. When she returned, she found him talking to Mrs. Miller. Carla groaned. Mrs. Miller was the biggest gossip in the whole congregation. She also had a heart to match her mouth, so everyone overlooked her gossip.

Still, Carla didn't want the older woman to get her hooks into Sam. She needn't have worried. Sam parried Mrs. Miller's questions with practiced ease and actually had the old lady giggling like a schoolgirl.

"How'd you do that?" Carla asked when Mrs. Miller finally left, declaring she had to see an old friend.

"Easy. I just told her she'd make a great TV journalist. It's the truth. She's got a reporter's instincts — goes right for the jugular."

Carla gave a rueful smile. "Don't I know it."

Sam grabbed her hand. "C'mon."

"Where?"

"I entered us in the three-legged race."

"You what?"

"The three-legged race. I hope you're fast. First prize is a carton of chocolate ice cream." He rolled his eyes. "I love chocolate."

"Is food all you ever think of?"

He sobered. "No. I think about you. A lot."

That wasn't the answer she'd expected. But then Sam didn't do the expected. He proved that now as he knelt beside her and bound their legs together with a length of rope provided by Mr. Porter, who was manning the booth.

Sam's hands were warm on her leg, and Carla was glad she'd worn her jeans instead of the dress she'd originally planned to wear.

"Are the contestants ready?" Mr. Porter asked.

He was greeted by a chorus in the affirmative. He raised his hand. "On your mark. Get set. Go!"

With their legs tied together and their arms wrapped around each other, Carla and Sam took off. They kept pace with most of the other contestants until she stumbled, dragging Sam down with her. He helped her up, but they now lagged far behind the others. They hobbled toward the finish line, laughing so hard they could barely stand.

Sam and Carla collapsed on the grass after crossing the finish line and watched as two small girls stepped forward to accept their prize.

"Beaten," Sam said between gasps for air. "By two little kids. I'll never live this down."

"Maybe they were ringers."

He brightened. "You mean midgets brought in to fix the race?"

She kept her face straight. "Why not?"

"Yeah. Why not?" He let his gaze travel over her face. Her cheeks were flushed, her eyes bright with excitement, her lips slightly parted. "You're something else, Reverend Stevens. Remind me to ask for you as my partner again."

"Even after I caused us to lose the race?"

"From where I'm sitting, we won." He leaned over, brushing his lips across her cheek.

She darted a look around them. Her congregation was fairly liberal, but she didn't think they were liberal enough to accept their minister being kissed right there on the church lawn.

"It's all right," Sam said. "Everyone else left."

He was right. The others had departed, leaving only the two of them.

"I should go help," she said. "I'm on the serving committee."

"Is there any committee you're not on?"

She started to smile, then realized what his question implied. "Quite a few, actually." She stood, brushing grass off her jeans.

Sam followed her to the church basement where a line of people twisted back and forth upon itself.

Carla slipped behind the serving table and fished a ladle from where it had disappeared into a pot of chili. She looked up to find Sam beside her.

"You should get in line," she told him. "I'll probably be here for a while."

"I'm right where I want to be. Just tell me what I'm supposed to do."

"How are you at dishing out Jell-O?" She pointed to the pans of lime, cherry, and orange Jell-O, each studded with bits of fruit.

"I think I can handle it."

98

She gave him a spatula. "Get ready. We're about to be descended upon."

The people came, eager to share in the bounty of food which spilled across the table, but even more eager, Carla realized, to get an eyeful of the man their minister was dating.

She sent Sam a sympathetic glance, wondering if he knew he was about to be put on public display.

He knew, all right. The look he gave her was half resigned, half amused.

"Think I'll pass muster?" he whispered.

In his faded jeans and pink knit shirt, he more than passed. He looked terrific.

"You'll do."

She started ladling out bowls of chili, all the while keeping an eye on Sam. She needn't have worried. After a few false starts, he wielded the spatula like a pro, cutting and serving the Jell-O in neat squares.

"Where'd you find him?" Mrs. Harvey asked Carla. "He's a hunk."

Carla glanced at Sam. Had he heard? Mrs. Harvey was a dear, but she was notoriously hard of hearing. Vanity prevented her from wearing a hearing aid so she tended to shout all her remarks, assuming that others suffered from the same malady.

"He's just a friend," Carla whispered back.

"Honey, men who look like that aren't just friends." The older woman winked slyly and tapped Carla on the wrist with her spoon. "Don't let him get away. You're not getting any younger, you know."

Carla chanced another look at Sam. What she saw in his face confirmed her fears.

He grinned. "Don't worry. I'm not going anywhere." He looked at her critically. "You've still got a few good years left."

He had heard.

"I'm sorry —"

"Don't be. I'm glad someone here approves of me. Maybe she'll put in a good word for me."

They continued serving the food until they were relieved by an older couple who shooed Carla and Sam away.

"Take your young man and sit down," the wife told Carla. "I'll fill some plates and bring them to you."

Carla had long since given up explaining that Sam was not "her young man" and smiled gratefully. "Thanks."

She and Sam squeezed chairs in at one of the long tables. The food was plentiful but plain, and she wondered what Sam thought of it.

There was Mrs. Johnson's macaroni, cheese, and tuna casserole, Mrs. Miller's glazed carrots, Mrs. Pike's green beans topped with bacon, Mrs. Meadows' chili, Mrs. Sanders' chocolate cake, Mrs. Lancaster's pecan pie . . . The list went on and on.

Each lady had her own specialty, and each was eager to show it off. The good-natured rivalry was part and parcel of the potluck. An empty pan at the end of the evening signaled a success, while a nearly full pan was a cause for sympathetic glances.

"Thanks," Sam said when a plate, overflowing with food, was placed before him. "It looks great." He turned beseeching eyes toward Carla and whispered. "How am I supposed to eat all this?"

"You can't. Just make sure you try some of everything."

He picked up a drumstick from Mrs. Harvey's fried chicken, bit into it, then sighed in appreciation. "Delicious."

Carla glanced around, hoping Sam was aware that his reaction was being scrutinized by everyone present. She berated herself for not warning him sooner and only hoped he understood the importance of the next few minutes.

He followed the same procedure with all the foods squeezed onto his plate, sampling each one, and then declaring it to be delicious, scrumptious, mouth-watering, delectable . . . until she was sure he'd run out of adjectives.

Finally, he pushed back his plate and made a show of loosening his belt several notches. "I haven't eaten this much good food since. . . . I take that back. I've *never* eaten this much good food before. And I've eaten in some of the finest restaurants there are."

The ladies hovering around him preened and basked in the praise.

When they dispersed, Sam leaned over to Carla. "I was telling the truth. Everything was wonderful. But I may never move again."

She patted his arm. "You made their day. Thank you."

"I'm flattered that my opinion is so important, but what I don't understand is why."

"You're *new*."

"That's it?"

"That's it." Seeing that he still didn't understand, she added, "Everyone else has been coming to these things for years. When I first got here, I had to make sure I didn't take any more of Mrs. Harvey's chicken than I did of Mrs. Lancaster's pecan pie. Let me tell you, I made a few blunders until I caught on."

"It's a wonder you don't look like Mrs. Sanders now," he said, "if you'd been eating like this for years."

Carla squelched a smile. Mrs. Sanders weighed at least two hundred pounds and was proud of it.

"After the first couple of times, everyone lost interest because I wasn't new anymore. Understand?"

"I'm beginning to. If I come to a few more of these things, no one will care how much I eat because I won't be new any longer. Right?"

"Right."

The shuffling of chairs interrupted what she was about to say next, and she looked around. "I'm on duty."

"Again?"

"Cleanup duty."

"Don't you ever quit?"

She smiled at him. "Why don't you sit back and relax? I'll take care of this and then we can go. Or if you want to leave now, I can catch a ride."

"No way. I'm under orders from Maude. Lead me to it."

She surveyed the tables, each holding piles of dirty dishes. "You're sure?"

"I'm sure."

"Thanks. It shouldn't be too bad. There're five others on the cleanup committee."

Carla started clearing the tables. By the time she reached the kitchen, only Sam remained.

"Where is everybody?"

"I sent them home. We don't need them."

"Have you ever washed a hundred dishes before?"

He looked unrepentantly cheerful. "No."

She sighed. "I was afraid of that."

"Do I get to wear an apron?"

Carla watched as Sam tackled the first stack of dirty dishes. With a frilly apron tied around his waist and his arms up to the elbows in soapsuds, he shouldn't have looked so appealing . . . so masculine. He should have looked ridiculous. Instead, he was more handsome than ever, the ruffles enhancing his masculinity rather than detracting from it. The direction of her thoughts disturbed her, and she made short work of the remaining dishes.

"You were pretty obvious tonight," Sam said.

"Obvious?"

104

"Come on, Carla. Wasn't that the idea? Make me realize you and I belong to different worlds."

"Yes." The plan had backfired, though. Sam fit in, charming the members of her congregation . . . and her. "I thought if you saw how different we were, you'd realize —"

"Realize what? That we come from different places? So what?"

"So what?"

"Yeah. So what? My parents made the so-called ideal marriage. They had everything in common — same background, same education, same expectations. Same everything. Everything except love."

"We're not talking about marriage."

"No, we're not. So why can't we see each other? As friends?" He didn't wait for her answer. "We have something special between us — something more important than the differences you feel bound to point out. Can't you feel it?"

"Yes . . . but it's happening too fast. I don't think —"

"Don't think. Just feel."

Sam kissed her. When he raised his head, Carla stared at him with bemused eyes.

It didn't matter that they were in a dingy basement, surrounded by piles of dirty dishes. It didn't matter that Sam wasn't her usual type of date. It didn't matter that their worlds were light-years apart.

All that mattered was how she felt in his arms.

After long moments had passed, she gently freed herself from the sweet warmth of his embrace.

He sighed. "This is neither the time nor the place."

"No," she agreed, "it isn't." She couldn't bring herself to tell him the truth — that she couldn't go on seeing him because she was afraid of risking her heart.

They finished cleaning up the kitchen, but the easy camaraderie they'd shared earlier was missing.

Sam took her home, as attentive as always, but she sensed he was far removed, in a world of his own. Perhaps, he too was having second thoughts.

In the rectory, she prepared for bed. Shaken by the kiss and her response to it, she stayed awake far into the night. Sam was getting too close, making her feel things she thought were long buried.

Not since the breakup with her fiancé had she allowed herself to feel anything for a man. Even now, four years later, she could remember the pain. Jeff had wanted her to give up her ministry once they were married. She'd tried to convince him that this wasn't just a job, it was a calling.

He wanted a wife, a helpmate, he'd told her. He'd almost convinced her until she realized what he really wanted was a hostess for parties as he entertained his business associates. He hadn't wanted a wife, he'd wanted a Barbie doll.

She'd shed her tears in private and vowed to never be that vulnerable again.

After resigning from the church in the affluent suburb where she'd served for two years, she accepted the pulpit of an inner-city church. She'd expected to work hard and long. What she hadn't expected was to fall in love with the rundown neighborhood and its proud residents.

Together, they were rebuilding the neighborhood. And they were making progress, she thought proudly. Most of the residents were older, retired people who refused to leave their homes despite the decay of their surroundings. But an influx of young families, attracted by the renovation efforts and cheap prices, was injecting new life into the neighborhood.

Carla felt needed here, something she'd missed in her old job. She had built a life here, one she was proud of.

Sam didn't fit in with any of her plans.

"Sam, what are you doing to me?" she whispered.

Only the sigh of the wind answered her.

Sam didn't like the way she'd been avoiding his gaze ever since he'd arrived that evening. She'd called him earlier, inviting him over for dessert and coffee. Carla had something to tell him. Of that, he was certain.

He was equally certain he wasn't going to like it. He had a pretty good idea what it was about. Her next words confirmed it.

After serving thick wedges of chocolate cake, she twisted a strand of hair between her fingers. "I don't think we should see each other anymore."

He was right. He didn't like it. He didn't like it at all. "Why?" He pushed aside his plate.

She spread her hands. "We'd never have met if it hadn't been for the race."

"But we *did* meet. I like you, Carla Stevens. I like you a lot. And I think you like me. Isn't it worth seeing where that takes us?"

"Where can it take us?"

He heard the fear in her voice. She was frightened at where they were heading.

Well, so was he. But he was willing to take a risk to find out.

"I don't know. But I want to find out. I *need* to find out." Hearing himself, he realized he'd never said anything more true. "Give me a chance. Give *us* a chance."

"I . . . can't."

"Can't or won't?"

"I don't know." She shook her head. "I'm sorry, Sam."

"So am I, sweetheart. So am I."

He hadn't tried to change her mind after that. He'd known all along that he and Carla were miles apart in their outlooks on life as well as their backgrounds.

It was for the best.

The only problem was that he was having a hard time convincing himself of it.

Chapter Six

That had been seven days ago.

Seven days.

One hundred and sixty-eight hours.

Each had dragged by with a slowness that tried his patience and tested his resolve to stay away from Carla.

He'd gone through the motions of campaigning, but his heart wasn't in it. His heart was somewhere in the streets, in the tenements, in the church . . . wherever Carla was.

Apparently, Jerry sensed it, for he poked Sam in the arm during their weekly strategy meeting.

"Listen, Sam, the election's in two weeks — two weeks to convince the voters that you're the best man for the job."

"I'm not the best man. I'm *a* man," Sam said wearily. He was getting tired of Jerry's constant harping.

"Sam, Sam, don't you get it? You're what this city needs. You can make a difference. You can do something to help all the people out there who need someone on their side." He waved an arm toward the window where Sam's office overlooked the streets.

Sam crossed the room to look out. From here, the people were toy-sized. But even at this distance, he could feel the urgency, the need, as they moved through their day. Naive as it sounded, he wanted to make things better.

Some of his annoyance slipped away. "I'd like to think so," he said, thinking of the welfare apartments, the county hospital, all the other things that needed someone to work toward making conditions better. "There's a lot to be done."

"And you're the man who can do it." Jerry clapped Sam on the back. "But first we've got to get you elected. The name of the game's exposure." Jerry gave Sam a speculative look. "You still seeing the lady minister?"

"Whether I am or not, it doesn't belong in the campaign."

"Sam, don't you get it? You let yourself open when you decided to run. Anything you do is public property. Seeing a lady minister, especially one involved with the homeless issue, is good PR."

"I didn't see Carla Stevens for good PR," Sam said in distaste. "I asked her out because I like her." It was a lot more than liking, but he wasn't about to admit that to Jerry.

"Sure, sure. I know that. But that doesn't mean we can't use it to our advantage."

For the first time, Sam was grateful he and Carla were no longer seeing each other. He didn't want her used as a publicity gimmick.

Jerry spread his hands. "I didn't make the rules. I just play by them. And so will you, if you want to get elected and stay in office."

"No." The word hung in the air.

"Look, Sam, you're a good guy, but you're being incredibly naive if you think you can run for office and not play the game."

"That's the difference between us, Jerry. I don't see this as a game."

"No, I don't guess you do. But that's why the city needs you." He snapped his fingers. "That's it. We'll play up your integrity, your old-fashioned values, and —"

"Jerry, I've got an idea."

"Great. What is it?"

"Why don't we let the issues speak for themselves? The people know where I stand. Let's give them credit to make up their own minds."

"Sam, you're crazy." Jerry was shaking his head. "Certifiable."

"You're probably right."

Sam watched as his campaign manager walked off, scratching his head, muttering something about dreamers and fools.

More and more frequently, Sam was regretting his decision to make Jerry Ross his campaign manager. Jerry was a good manager, but he'd lost all perspective in his desire to see Sam win the election.

He supposed he should be grateful that Jerry was so devoted, but right now all Sam wanted was for the election to be over. He was tired of the speeches, the rallies, the hand-shakes, the everlasting smiling when that was the last thing he felt like doing was smiling.

If only he could talk with Carla. She'd know what to do. But she'd made it pretty clear that she didn't want to see him again.

He slammed his fist into his hand. To heck with what she wanted. He'd played by her rules; now it was time he started making some of his own.

Idly, he looked at his calendar. It was Sunday. He knew where Carla would be.

Organ music drifted through the chapel. Sam could feel himself responding to the quiet tug at his senses. He hadn't been inside a church in years.

He slipped into a pew on the back row. He recognized several of the people from the potluck dinner and saw the speculative glances thrown his way. Some were distinctly unfriendly. Probably the whole congregation knew he and Carla were no longer seeing each other and blamed him.

Well, so be it.

He forced a smile to his lips and squared his shoulders.

He'd faced sneering opponents, hostile reporters, and sarcastic journalists, but the disapproving looks directed his way by Mrs. Miller and gang had him quaking in his boots.

The music stopped, and Carla took her place behind the pulpit. Sunlight filtering through a stained-glass window framed her in a rainbow of colors.

"Good morning," she said, her voice strong and vibrant.

Murmured "good mornings" were returned.

"In another month, we'll be celebrating Thanksgiving, a day designated to give thanks for our blessings. We'll eat turkey and stuffing and pumpkin pies. We'll watch the parades on TV and fall asleep during a football game."

Appreciative chuckles rippled through the congregation.

"But there are others here in our city who aren't as fortunate. They'll be lucky if they have a bowl of soup at a shelter."

She paused, letting her words take effect, Sam realized.

"Most of us have never known real want, never known what it means to go to bed hungry and wake up hungry, or, even worse, hear our children cry because they're hungry. We have in our own community a shelter that desperately needs donations — money, food, anything you can spare.

"We can't claim to love our neighbors on Sunday if we ignore those same people the rest of the week."

Murmured "amens" punctuated her words as members of the congregation nodded in agreement.

"If we truly believe what we say we do, then we must be prepared to —" Her voice faltered, and she stumbled over the next words as her gaze found Sam's. "— to give, not just of our means but of our time, ourselves. The shelter needs volunteers. It needs you and me. *You* can make a difference. *I* can make a difference. All it takes is one person who's willing to care."

One person . . . one voice.

Sam remembered the first time she'd challenged him with those words. He heard the passion in her voice, the conviction, the fervor. He touched his cheeks, surprised to find they were wet. He was crying.

"Our chorister will lead us in a hymn now," Carla said.

Sam reached into his pocket and pulled out a handkerchief. Sniffles, blowing of noses, and quiet crying provided a counterpoint to the strains of the organ.

Carla had touched these people, he realized. She had touched *him.*

After the service closed with a prayer, he watched as she threaded her way through the congregation to stand near the door. There, she shook hands with the people as they filed out. Sam waited his turn, watching, listening to her. She had a kind word, a soft smile, for everyone.

When he closed his hand over hers, he felt the tremor.

"Good morning, Mr. Hastings," she said, color staining her cheeks pink.

He resisted the urge to smile. She was using her "minister's voice" on him. Two could play at this game.

116

"Good morning, Reverend Stevens. Wonderful sermon." He lowered his voice. "You're even more beautiful than I remember."

The color in her cheeks deepened. He'd flustered her. A good sign. Maybe then he could convince her that she needed him in her life. He already knew that he needed her in his.

"Ah . . . thank you. If you'll excuse me. . . ." She turned her attention to the next person in line, but Sam didn't move on.

Instead, he stayed by her side, talking with members of the congregation. His hand slipped behind her to rest on the small of her back. He felt her startled awareness, heard her quick intake of breath.

She wasn't indifferent to him. As much as she'd tried to convince him that she was, he knew better. The knowledge bolstered his courage, and he weathered the frankly curious gazes of members of the congregation as they filed past. He liked that they felt protective of Carla. Now all he had to do was to convince them — and her — that she didn't need protecting from him.

Finally, the last one had gone. Now that he was alone with her, he wasn't sure how to begin.

As usual, Carla didn't waste time. "Why did you come?"

"I wanted to see you." That wasn't the truth — at least, not the whole truth. "I *had* to see you."

"Oh."

"Yeah. Oh. I liked your sermon. Words come alive when you say them with all that passion."

"Thank you." She hesitated. "I'm glad you came."

"May I walk you home?"

"I . . . okay."

"I tried to stay away," he said as he helped her lock up.

"I know. I've missed you."

"Good." He couldn't quite keep the satisfaction from his voice. "Don't send me away again."

"I won't . . . I can't."

The little hitch in her voice did funny things to his heart. "We have something special between us, Carla. You feel it, don't you?"

"Yes. Only . . . I'm afraid."

"Don't be. Just let it happen."

Sam sealed their new beginning with a kiss, a kiss that promised all the things he couldn't say — yet. Reluctantly, he released her.

"I won't promise not to want you. I wouldn't be human if I didn't. But I won't push you into something you're not ready for."

"Where are we heading, Sam?"

"I don't know. But I think it's worth finding out. Don't you?"

"Y-yes. I do."

He waited while she slipped on her coat. Outside, they braced themselves against the cold. Ocher, saffron, and amber leaves caught the sun and held it, a glittering mist of gold as they danced in the breeze.

Sam tucked her under his arm, holding her close beside him. "Okay if I'll call tonight?" he asked when they reached her house.

"I'd like that."

Sam walked back to the church where he'd left his car, his step lighter than it had been in a week. His troubles with Jerry, the extra work piled up at the office, all seemed to fade.

Because of Carla.

Shoving the papers to a back corner of his desk, Sam stretched and yawned. He'd put in a good five hours catching up on work. Now he wanted to relax. At one time, he'd have flipped on the television

119

and found a movie. But not any longer.

Because of work schedules — his and hers — he hadn't seen Carla since Sunday. They'd talked on the phone every night though, at first sharing the events of their days. The conversations had gradually grown more intimate until they were now sharing thoughts and feelings.

He knew she was probably tired after leading an evening study group, so he didn't intend to keep her on the phone for a long time. He just wanted to hear her voice.

He smiled, thinking she could make a fortune if she bottled that voice. Its soft tones had a way of cutting through his worries and dissolving them.

He let the phone ring again and again.

After dialing the church and getting no answer, he looked up the hospital's number and asked for Maude's room.

Maude brushed away his questions about her health and cut to the matter at hand.

"You called here looking for Carla, didn't you?"

There was no point in lying. "Yes."

"Well, she's not here. Have you tried the church? She sometimes stays in her office there, catching up on paperwork."

"I already tried the church."

"Well, then, she's likely downtown."

"It's freezing out."

Maude clucked. "That's why she's there. Giving out blankets and coffee to the street people."

Sam curbed what he'd been about to say. She had no business being out late at night by herself in the downtown area.

"Give me street names," he said, trying to hide his growing worry.

Maude rattled off the names of several streets where he might find Carla. He forced himself to thank Maude politely before hanging up and pulling on a jacket.

An hour later, he was still driving up and down streets, looking for Carla's rattletrap of a car. When he spotted it, he breathed a sigh of relief.

He found her handing out blankets and coffee just as Maude had predicted. He maneuvered his way through the throng of people and looped an arm around her shoulders, hugging her to him.

"Sam." She flashed a smile at him. "What are you doing here?"

"Looking for you. C'mon."

"Where?"

"I'm taking you home."

"I can't go. Not yet."

Sam bit back the impatient words that threatened to spill over. "It's freezing out here. Let me take you home."

"I'm not going anywhere until I finish here."

He'd just spent an hour looking for her, scared out of his mind that something had happened to her. He was cold, tired, and out of patience. "You're finished."

She raised her chin and shrugged off his arm. "Sam, I appreciate you coming to look for me, but as you can see, I'm perfectly all right. And you've got no right interfering in my work." Her voice softened. "Now, if you'll excuse me, I've got work to do."

Misty plumes of cold air framed her face as she spoke, a silent reminder of the frigid temperature that was dropping even as they talked.

"I thought caring about you gave me that right." He fitted a finger under her chin so that her gaze met his. "Was I wrong?"

"You weren't wrong, but I can't stop what I'm doing here." She brushed a cold-reddened hand across his jaw. "Not even for you."

"Why do you have to be the one handing out food and blankets?" He ran a hand through his hair. "You can't save the world by yourself. Aren't there others who could do this?"

"If I don't do my part, how can I ask others to help?"

"Your business is saving souls, not risking your neck to feed them."

"I can't save souls when their bodies are starving."

"You need a keeper." He regretted the words as soon as they were out of his mouth and started to apologize when she stopped him.

"It's lucky I'm not asking for your approval." She lifted her chin a notch higher.

"If you think I'm going to let you wander around the streets at night, you're even more naive than I thought."

"How are you going to stop me?"

He tried a different tactic. "Why do you have to do this all by yourself?" he asked, gesturing to the sacks of food and blankets that surrounded her. "Aren't there others who can help?"

"Not many people want to come to this part of town."

"I don't blame 'em," he muttered.

"Neither do I. But that doesn't change what needs to be done."

"What's so important that you have to be down here in the middle of the night?

Let me take you home, and we'll come back first thing in the morning. What difference is a few hours going to make?"

"Look around you, Sam. Take a hard look."

Sam let his gaze take in the scene before him. A small girl huddled close to her mother, with only a blanket shared between them to shield them against the caustic bite of the wind. An old man cupped his hands around a Styrofoam cup of coffee, the steam haloing his uncovered head. Two teenage girls eagerly accepted the sandwiches Carla handed them.

He swallowed hard. She was right. These people needed help *now.* Not when it was daylight, not when it was safe, not when it was convenient — but now.

He was shamed by his tunnel vision. Oh, sure, he could make excuses, telling himself he was worried about Carla. But the truth was, never once had he bothered to look around him.

Once again, he was humbled by her willingness to do what had to be done, despite the risks involved.

He had blindly assumed he had all the answers. But there were more questions than answers.

"What can I do to help?"

She gave him a searching look. "Here,"

she said and handed him a thermos of coffee. "Start refilling the cups. It's instant, but at least it's hot."

"Where are you going?"

"I want to see those girls," she said, pointing to the teenagers he'd noticed earlier. "They look like runaways. Maybe I can convince them to go back home . . . before it's too late."

Sam didn't have to ask her what she meant by that. The city was full of boys and girls who had left home, looking for something better in the excitement of the city. Only that something better never existed.

He watched as she approached the two young girls. They looked scared, ready to bolt at the slightest provocation. He couldn't hear what Carla said to them, but he saw her slip her hand into her pocket and pull out several bills. She pressed them into the hand of one of the girls.

He shouldn't have been surprised. He already knew that Carla had more than her share of compassion.

"You gave them money," he said when she rejoined him.

She nodded. "A little. They agreed to go back home. They needed bus fare."

"How do you know they'll use it for that?"

"They gave me their word. That's good enough for me."

Torn between wanting to lecture her on her naivete and kiss her for her generosity, he did neither. He simply drew her into his arms and held her. "You're cold."

She shivered again. "I guess you're right."

It was only then he noticed she wasn't wearing a coat. "Where's your coat?"

"I don't have one."

"I can see that. What happened to it?"

"Maybe I didn't bring one."

He wasn't buying that. "What did you do with it?"

Her gaze shifted away from his. Gently, he caught her face between his palms, compelling her to look at him.

"What did you do with it?" he repeated gently, though he was pretty sure he knew the answer.

"I gave it to a woman. She was coughing so badly she could barely stand. I wanted to take her to the hospital, but she wouldn't let me. So I gave her my coat. I'm not that cold," she said and immediately negated the words by shivering again. "I have other coats," she said when he continued to stare at her. "She needed one.

Anyone would have done the same thing."

Not anyone, Sam thought. *Only Carla.*

He shrugged off his suede jacket and settled it over her shoulders. It swallowed her, but it provided some protection from the wind that whipped around them. By now she was shivering so much she could barely slip her arms into it.

"I can't take your coat."

"I'll be all right. I've got a sweater on. It's you I'm worried about. What am I going to do with you?" he murmured, rubbing his hands up and down her arms.

"Help me hand out these," she said, gesturing to the supplies she'd brought.

"You can't be serious. You're so cold now you can barely move. Let me take you home. I'll come back and finish up."

"I can't leave yet."

"At least wait in the truck."

She smiled and shook her head. "With two of us, it'll go faster."

Seeing that she wasn't about to change her mind, Sam helped her give out the rest of the sandwiches and blankets. Though he wanted to speed things up and hustle her home where she could start to thaw out, she refused to be rushed and had a kind word, and an encouraging smile for each of the people who shuffled forward.

By now he was shivering too, but he kept going. All the while his admiration for Carla was growing. The lady had guts — more than anyone he'd ever met.

When the last of the supplies had been given away, Sam wrapped an arm around her waist. "Come on," he said, and guided her to his truck.

"My car —"

"We'll get it tomorrow."

Sam drove quickly, chancing a glance at Carla when he could. Her shivering eventually subsided as the heater filled the car's interior with warmth. Her soft, even breathing told him she was asleep.

At her house, he shook her gently. "C'mon, sleepyhead. Time to get out. We're home."

She murmured something and pushed his hands away.

"Okay. We'll do it your way." He slid an arm beneath her knees and the other around her shoulders. At the door, he paused while he searched her purse for her key. Finding it, he opened the door.

Inside, he carried her to the sofa. After settling her there, he removed his jacket from her, tucked an afghan over her, and then headed to the kitchen. In a few minutes, he returned, carrying a steaming cup on a tray. He set the tray on the coffee table and gently shook her awake.

Her hair tumbled about her face, and her eyes were soft and dreamy as she looked up at him. "Sam? Where are we?"

"Home. Drink this," he said, wrapping her hands around the mug of cocoa.

She managed a few sips. "Thanks."

He sat beside her, making sure she finished all of it.

"That was wonderful," she said.

"Hot chocolate should never be served without marshmallows, but I couldn't find any." He gave her a long look. "As a matter of fact, I couldn't find much of anything in your cabinets or refrigerator."

She avoided his gaze. "I haven't had time to go to the store."

"You're so busy feeding everyone else, you don't have time to shop for food." He heard the censure in his voice and knew she'd resent it.

He was right.

"I was going to go to the store tomorrow."

He set the cup aside and pulled her up. "Come on. It's time for you to go to bed. You're dead on your feet."

"I'm going right now."

"You're sure?"

"I'm sure." As he started to leave, she touched his arm. "Sam?"

"Yeah?"

"Thanks. For everything."

He brushed his lips against hers. "I'm glad I could help. Get some sleep. And the next time you decide to deliver food in the middle of the night, call me." He tilted her chin up. "Promise?"

"Promise."

"I'll see you tomorrow," he said and let himself out.

Alone now, Carla reflected on Sam's reaction. He'd been angry, all right. But it had been *for* her, not *at* her. It'd been a long time since anyone cared what happened to her. Warmed by his concern, she admitted what she'd run from for too long.

Commitment.

Ever since her fiancé left her, she'd shied away from involvement. Sam was breaching the wall she'd erected around her heart, chipping away at her defenses with slow but sure strokes.

A tiny smile hovered at her lips. Warm and caring, strong yet gentle, he made her feel cherished. Her smile dimmed as she realized the implications. She was falling in love with Sam. But was love enough to bridge the differences between them?

Absently, she stroked his jacket where he'd tossed it on the back of the sofa and then forgotten it. The suede was warm and supple beneath her fingers. She lifted it to her face and inhaled deeply. It bore the scent of the pine after-shave he favored, and another, subtler aroma. She puzzled over it, until she realized that the jacket smelled of Sam himself. She'd return it to him tomorrow.

She was smiling as she got ready for bed. It was Saturday. Maybe they could spend the day together. She fell asleep, a tiny smile still on her lips.

The sound of pounding on the door woke her. She glanced at the clock. Eight a.m. Who'd be knocking at her door at this time of morning?

She grabbed her robe and tied it about her waist as she went to open the door.

Sam stood there, his hands full of cartons and containers. "May I come in?"

She stepped back, holding the door open for him. "Of course." Surreptitiously, she smoothed her hair and wondered if her face had sleep wrinkles.

Sam headed to the kitchen.

"What's all this?" she asked, following him.

"Breakfast." He tugged at a curl. "Get dressed in old clothes. As soon as we eat, we're going out."

"Where?"

"You'll see."

She pulled on jeans and a sweatshirt and then dragged a brush through her hair. Sam was pouring orange juice as she walked back into the kitchen.

"Hope you like doughnuts," he said, passing a box to her.

"Love 'em. Especially chocolate ones that get all over my fingers and I have to lick it off."

"My kind of woman."

As they ate, Carla studied Sam. He looked happy and relaxed. He also looked like a man with a secret.

"Where did you say we were going?"

"It's a surprise." The smug grin on his face told her he wasn't saying anything more.

Carla felt a matching grin tickle her lips. She loved surprises.

He helped her rinse the dishes and then held out his hand. "Ready?"

"Ready." She put her hand in his. "I just wish I knew what I was ready for."

"How are you at painting?"

"Pretty good, I guess. What are we going to be painting?"

"Ethan and Maude's house."

"What?"

"I stopped by to visit Maude a couple of nights ago. Ethan told me he'd been planning on painting the house before her fall. I thought we'd surprise them."

Fifteen minutes later, they pulled up in front of the Sandbergs' home. Carla looked at the clapboard house, its once-yellow paint chipped and peeling.

"Don't worry," Sam said. "I know we can't do the whole thing by ourselves. I've got some men coming in to work on it tomorrow. They'll sand and paint. I thought we could do the trim work, though."

She leaned across the stick shift to kiss him. "You're a nice man."

"Only nice?" He looked affronted. "This is all part of my campaign to convince you that I'm wonderful."

"You're wonderful."

"Does wonderful rate another kiss?"

"I'll let you know when we're done."

Whistling softly, Sam hauled a ladder, paint, brushes, and tarps from his truck. "I thought we'd start at the back of the house."

"Why not the front?"

"We'll get better as we go, and the front will get our best work."

It should have been dull, Carla thought, painting eaves and trim. But not with Sam. When she wasn't looking, he swiped his brush down her nose, leaving a yellow stripe. When she tried to wipe it away, he took the rag from her and did it for her. The small gesture warmed her as did the look in his eyes, a look that promised there'd be more days like this one.

It was one of those late fall days that had forgotten the seasonal clock, a throwback to early autumn when the air was crisp rather than cold. Sunlight slanted through trees stripped bare, casting dappled patterns across the ground. Leaves crunched underfoot, a carpet of red and gold and brown.

By the end of the morning, they'd completed the back and one side of the house's trim.

"Break time," he called.

She pushed back her hair and gave an exaggerated groan. "Thank heavens. I thought you were going to work us straight through the day."

"Do I look like a slave driver?"

She cocked her head to one side. "I don't know. What does a slave driver look like?"

He pulled his eyebrows together and assumed a fierce expression. "Like this."

She only laughed, causing him to look fiercer than ever.

He pulled a cooler out of the back of his truck and produced chicken, potato salad, and dill pickles from the deli. They took their time eating, enjoying the food and each other's company.

"We'd better get back to work," Sam said, putting the leftovers back into the cooler. "I've got a strategy meeting with Jerry tonight. He thinks we need a media blitz before the election."

"You'll win without that," she said.

"I wish Jerry shared your confidence."

She grimaced in distaste. She'd only met the man once, but he'd come across as pushy and full of himself.

"Jerry has that effect on some people," Sam said. "But he's an all-right guy. He's worked plenty hard for me."

"Was it for you?"

Sam frowned. "What do you mean?"

"Just that he strikes me as someone who's looking out for himself."

"You're wrong. Jerry may be a little over-enthusiastic, but he'd never cross the line."

"I hope you're right."

"Jerry's a friend. He wouldn't do anything to hurt me."

By unspoken agreement, they changed the subject.

As Sam had predicted, their work improved as they went along. Carla was almost sorry when they'd reached the front of the house and were nearly done.

He gathered up the brushes and washed them out under the hose while she stood back to admire their efforts.

"I think it looks pretty good," she said.

"It's nice to know I have another profession to fall back on." He checked his watch. "I'd like to take you to dinner, but I've got to get home and change before meeting with Jerry."

Sam pushed away his own misgivings about Jerry as a campaign manager. He felt disloyal even considering the idea of firing Jerry. But, like a nagging toothache, Carla's words wouldn't go away.

"I thought you said you and the lady minister were on the outs," Jerry said two hours later as he and Sam wrapped up the details on a radio announcement.

"We're friends, Jerry, friends — that's all."

"Sure. Sure. But why'd you keep it a secret?"

Sam tried to ignore the reproach in

136

Jerry's voice. "I didn't think it was important."

"Anything about you is important. Don't you know that?"

Sam picked up the latest voter poll and pretended to study it, hoping Jerry would take the hint and let it go.

Only later that evening did he pause over Jerry's interest in his friendship with Carla. Jerry hadn't meant anything. He knew how Sam felt about using Carla or his relationship with her to get votes.

By the time he saw the papers the next morning, it was too late.

Chapter Seven

Councilman Hopeful Woos Ordained Minister. . . . Sam kept reading, his temper heating with every word.

Strictly speaking, the article didn't contain anything that wasn't true. It mentioned his participation in the charity race, his contribution to Everyone Deserves a Home, his visit to the welfare apartments.

But it implied a lot more, making it sound like Sam had been instrumental in developing the idea for a community home and was now spearheading it to completion. It was an insult to all those who had worked hard to raise funding and interest in the community home.

The whole thing smacked of Jerry's touch. Sam's lips tightened as he reread the part about Carla.

She'd hate this. He didn't find it strange that his first concern should be for her. The campaign no longer mattered if it hurt her.

Even as he read, he reached for the phone

and punched out her number. With any luck, she hadn't seen the paper yet. Maybe he could warn her before she read the article.

"Carla, it's Sam —"

"Councilman Hastings. How nice to hear from you."

He flinched at her sarcasm. *He was too late.*

"It's not what you think. I swear to you I didn't have anything —"

"I'm sorry, Sam. I know it wasn't you. I shouldn't have snapped at you like that."

The anger had drained from her voice, and he breathed a sigh of relief. He couldn't change what had happened, but at least Carla didn't blame him for it. He felt as though a great weight had been lifted. He'd deal with Jerry later.

"I should be the one apologizing."

"What for? It was Jerry, wasn't it?"

He didn't answer directly. "It's my responsibility."

"You didn't do anything wrong, Sam."

"That's just it. I didn't do anything. If I had, this wouldn't have happened. I should have listened to you."

"You believed in your friend. It's not your fault he didn't deserve your loyalty."

Her voice, soft as a summer rain, washed over him, absolving him of guilt.

"Will this cause problems for you?" he asked.

"I don't think so. The publicity might even help the community home."

He could hear the smile in her voice now and knew it was for his benefit. Once again he was reminded of her generosity of spirit. She'd been used, their relationship had been used, but she'd managed to turn it into something positive.

"What are you going to do?" Her voice had sobered, forcing his attention back to what needed to be done.

"Get rid of Jerry for starters. Get the paper to print a retraction."

"Why?"

"Because he used you, used us."

"I understand that. What I meant was, why have the paper print a retraction?"

He paused, surprised at the question. "I thought that's what you'd want."

"I'm not ashamed of our relationship, Sam," she said quietly.

"Neither am I. I just don't want it used as a votegetter."

"Neither do I. But it's done now. And the paper can't retract something if it's true, can they?"

"No, they can't."

"Sam?"

"Yeah?"

"Thank you."

"For what?"

"For caring how I feel."

"Don't you know how important you are to me, Carla?" he asked in a low voice.

"I'm beginning to."

He hung up a few minutes later and read through the story again. He reached for the phone.

"Jerry, you're fired."

Without a manager, Sam started handling the campaign — or what was left of it — as he'd wanted to from the beginning.

He called a radio station and asked for airtime. The night of the broadcast, he phoned Carla, needing to hear her voice.

"You'll be great," she said.

Her quiet confidence filled him with warmth. His earlier nervousness vanished as he waited for his introduction.

"Too many of us are waiting for the government, the church, *someone else* to take care of the problem." He paused, letting his words sink in. "Well, it's not going to happen. We have to help — you and me. The homeless situation isn't going to go away simply by throwing money at it."

Carla listened to the broadcast, tears streaming down her face. Sam *did* care.

Feeling so proud she could burst, she drove to the station and waited for him outside.

When Sam emerged, he was surrounded by reporters all shooting questions at him. She edged closer, wanting to hear his answers.

"Mr. Hastings, can you tell us how you mean to help the homeless of our city?" a newspaper columnist asked.

"First, by supporting the community home a local organization is working to have built. Second, by making people see this is everyone's problem," he responded.

"That's all well and good, but exactly *how* are you going to carry out those goals?"

"By asking everyone to help."

The reporter smirked. "You really think that's going to work?"

Sam leveled a hard gaze at the young woman. "It will if we start thinking with our hearts as well as with our heads."

"What about funding from the city?"

"If I'm elected to the City Council, I intend to push for a bigger budget to help build the community home that so many people have worked toward. But money alone isn't the answer. It's going to take all of us if we're going to make a difference. Someone once told me that it starts with one person, one voice. I want to be that voice for our city."

Carla's heart swelled with love as she listened to him. He truly did understand. She waited until the reporters had dispersed and Sam was alone before joining him.

"You heard the broadcast?" he asked.

She nodded.

"What did you think?"

"I think you're going to make a great city councilman." She hugged his arm and rested her cheek against it.

Two days later, her words were proved true. Though all the tallies weren't completed by late evening of election day, it was clear Sam had won.

The following morning, Carla read the headline of the local newspaper with satisfaction: *Hastings Wins by Large Margin*. She smiled, remembering Sam's speech on the radio. He'd make a difference in the city because he cared.

Her smile dimmed as she thought about tonight.

Pete Hammond, one of the council members, was throwing a party to celebrate Sam's victory. When Sam had asked her to go with him, she'd demurred, fearing she'd be out of place.

"You'll fit in wherever you are," he'd said. "Besides, I need you with me."

"You do?"

"To keep me from being bored stiff. Pete and Barbie Hammond throw the dullest parties in the state."

"Oh."

"I want you with me, Carla," he said, sliding the back of his finger across her cheek.

"Yes."

"Yes, what?"

"Yes, I'll go."

"You won't be sorry."

Carla prayed he was right.

That night, she'd changed clothes three times before putting on the dress she'd originally planned to wear, a burgundy velvet.

When the doorbell rang, she ran to answer it.

Sam took one look at her and gave a low whistle. "You look great."

"So do you."

In a tux, he was even more arresting

than normal. Carla wished it was just the two of them celebrating tonight. She and Sam had had precious little time together, especially during the last two weeks.

When Sam had fired Jerry, he'd had to take over all the manager's duties plus keep up with his own. She was honest enough to admit she'd missed him.

Some of what she was feeling must have shown in her face, for Sam drew her to him and kissed her lightly. "I know. I'd rather it be just the two of us. But . . ."

"It's all right."

Sam kissed her again. "We don't have to stay long," he promised.

"I don't mind. Honestly. As long as we're together."

She wondered just how truthful her words were when they were shown into the Hammond mansion thirty minutes later by a white-coated butler.

Laughter pierced the air. The scent of expensive perfume wafted around her, so cloying and heavy she could scarcely breathe. The clink of crystal and china competed with dozens of voices, raised to be heard over the band. The resulting din resembled the chatter of magpies.

She smiled at the analogy.

Jewel-toned dresses contrasted with dark

tuxes, a paint box of colors and a perfect backdrop for an evening devoted to excess.

They were all here, she thought. The wealthy and influential, the movers and shakers, the power brokers and those who benefited from that power. She put names to faces she'd seen only in newspapers.

Sam took her elbow, steering her toward a cluster of people.

"Carla, I'd like you to meet Councilman Hammond and his wife Barbie. Pete, Barbie, Reverend Carla Stevens."

Carla shook hands, aware of the raised eyebrows and subtle scrutiny directed her way by the councilman and his wife.

"It's nice to meet you," she murmured.

"Reverend, how good of you to come," Barbie Hammond said, barely touching Carla's hand.

"Yes, yes, good of you to come," her husband seconded.

"Reverend, will you forgive me if I steal Sam for a few minutes to meet someone?" Barbie asked, hooking her arm through his.

"Of course."

Sam gave Carla an apologetic look before Barbie led him away.

Carla turned to the councilman. "It's very generous of you to host the party for Sam."

The councilman preened a bit. "I told Barbie to pull out all the stops for tonight's bash. She knows how to throw a party."

Carla let her gaze travel around the room, nodding her agreement. "She must be very organized."

Pete Hammond laughed. "She should be. She's got two secretaries who do nothing but arrange things for her."

Not knowing how to respond to that, Carla simply nodded again. "Councilman, I'm glad to have a chance to talk with you."

He threw her a wary look. "Oh? Why is that?"

"It's about the community home. Perhaps Sam's mentioned it to you?"

"Yes, I believe he did. Sounds like a good thing."

"I'm glad you think so, because we could use your support."

"My support?"

"We hope to have enough money to buy land for the home soon. If the City Council approves matching what we've raised —"

"Now, just hold on a minute. We're talking about a lot of money here — a whole lot of money."

She needed to step carefully. "Councilman

Hammond, if you could see how over-crowded the shelters are, you'd know why the community home we want to build is so important."

"I've visited the downtown shelter. It looked very organized and efficient. The director told me they fed over a hundred a day."

She heard the pride in his voice, the smug tone that told her numbers, not people, would always come first.

"I think you're missing the point, Councilman. Those people are at the shelter because they have nowhere else to go. That's why we need —"

"You don't want us to tear down the shelter, do you?" he asked.

She bit back an impatient sigh. "Of course not. But shelters aren't the answer. They're a temporary solution. People need a place to live, not just a bed overnight."

"All these things cost money, Reverend, *taxpayers'* money. We have to take that into consideration as well. The good people who pay their taxes don't take kindly to having their money used to support able-bodied people. If these people had any ambition, they'd be out working, not waiting for a handout."

Carla tried to keep her words reasonable,

her tone even. She wouldn't accomplish anything by giving way to the anger that threatened to spill over at his callousness.

"Handouts are the last thing most people want. They want a chance to work, to take care of their families."

"Jobs are available."

"Have you ever tried looking for a job, Councilman, when you had nowhere to change clothes, to bathe, to brush your teeth?"

"Well, no, but that's not the point."

"It's exactly the point."

"You're emotional," he said, the patronizing tone in his voice grating on her nerves. "Natural enough in a woman."

"That's right, I'm emotional. But that doesn't mean I'm wrong."

He patted her hand. "You can't change the world."

Her control snapped. "That's the poorest excuse for doing nothing I've ever heard. If individuals don't do something, who will?"

"There are organizations designed to help these people."

"Who exactly are 'these people,' Councilman?" she asked, her voice dangerously quiet.

"People who . . . you know who I mean."

"No, I'm afraid I don't. Why don't you explain it to me?"

"People who can't hold a job. Drunks. That kind of people."

"Have you ever met a homeless person? Talked to one? Found out why he's on the streets?"

"Well . . . no."

"In other words, you don't have any idea of what you're talking about."

"Now just a minute, honey —"

"I'm not your honey, Councilman. I'm a minister. What's more, I'm someone who cares."

"Yes . . . yes . . . if you'll excuse me, I see someone I must talk to." Councilman Hammond turned away, his rotund body bobbing up and down in his haste to put as much distance as possible between them. If she hadn't felt so much like crying, it would have been funny.

Sam frowned, searching for Carla in the crowd of people. She'd been talking to Pete Hammond and then disappeared.

He'd sensed her uneasiness the minute they walked into the home, but he'd chalked it up to nerves. Now he knew it wasn't so simple. She seemed to have put up a barrier between them, one he didn't understand but was determined to bring down.

Then he saw her. Standing slightly apart from the rest, she appeared to be observing. He spent a few minutes just watching her. In her simple dress, with her hair pulled back at the neck and fastened with a satin bow, she stood out from the crowd.

It wasn't just her unaffected beauty, it was something more basic. It was the way she looked at life. Unlike almost everyone else here, she wasn't out to impress anyone.

He threaded his way through the clusters of people, smiling and shaking his head at those who wanted to detain him. He'd spent the last half hour listening to people who wanted to impress him; now he was doing what he wanted to do.

When he drew closer to Carla, he could see something was troubling her. Her smile was a little too wide, her eyes a little too bright as she looked up at him.

"What's wrong?" he asked.

"Nothing."

"C'mon, sweetheart, the truth. You're not having a good time, are you?" He stroked the inside of her wrist, hoping to help her relax.

"Who wouldn't have a good time at a party like this? The food's wonderful, the music great, the —" She stopped. "I'm sorry, Sam. I haven't had much experience with this kind of thing."

He didn't intend to let her off the hook. "I thought ministers always told the truth."

"All right. But, remember, you asked."

He grinned. "I'll remember."

"After she'd finished with you, Barbie Hammond cornered me. She's got all the personality of a postage stamp. All she can talk about is her latest shopping trip and how much weight she lost on her pickle and grapefruit diet."

Sam chuckled. "It was artichoke and grapefruit."

"You're right — artichokes and grapefruit. How could I have forgotten?"

"But that's not what's bothering you."

"No," she said, "it's not."

"Tell me."

"I tried to talk to Pete Hammond about the community home. After patting my hand and telling me I was naive, he told me the city had enough shelters. He couldn't get away fast enough."

"Sweetheart, not everyone has your social conscience. That doesn't make them bad people. Just different. So you don't like Barbie and Pete, but the rest aren't so bad."

"If you don't mind listening to them take potshots behind one another's backs."

"You're a little hard on them, aren't you?"

"It's the truth. If you'd take a good look, you'd see it for yourself."

"I didn't bring you here tonight to criticize my friends." He heard the stiffness in his voice and was reminded of his father. That was the last thing he wanted.

"Why *did* you bring me?" Carla asked quietly.

"I wanted you to meet them, see what they're like, start to feel comfortable —"

"You wanted me to fit in with them. You wanted me to become one of them, didn't you? I'm sorry, Sam, I can't. I don't even *want* to."

"You're twisting my words."

"Sam, take a look around. I don't fit in here. I almost wish I could, because I know it's important to you. I tried doing that four years ago for another man. I promised myself then I'd never try to be something I'm not."

"I'm not asking you to be something you're not."

"Aren't you?"

He thought about it. Maybe he was. "*You're* important to me."

"And you're important to me. You once told me I was putting up barriers because of the differences between us."

He nodded slowly. "I remember."

"My not fitting in here is one of those differences. It's up to you whether or not it's a barrier."

She was right. He had wanted her to fit in with his friends, be a part of his world. "I'm sorry."

"Don't be. I'm glad you brought me. But I think . . . Sam, what happens to all the leftover food?"

"Leftover food?" He tried — and failed — to make sense of the words.

"You know . . . the food that doesn't get eaten. There must be tons at a party like this." She grabbed his hand. "C'mon."

"Where are we going?"

"The kitchen."

Following one of the white-coated workers into the kitchen, Carla gasped. Dozens — hundreds — of finger sandwiches, hors d'oeuvres, cakes, and tarts were piled high on the counters.

"What happens to the leftovers?" Carla asked the man who appeared to be in charge.

The harried-looking man whirled on her. "What's the matter? Didn't you get enough?"

"I had plenty. Everything was delicious," she added.

Sam watched as the man relaxed.

He swiped at his forehead with the back of his hand. "I'm sorry, ma'am. I shouldn't have snapped at you. You won't tell the hostess, will you?"

"Of course not. It must have been a long night for you."

"You can say that again. That is . . . I mean . . ."

"It's all right. I understand." She smiled.

He looked considerably relieved. "Now, what were you asking about the leftovers?"

"I just wondered what happened to them?"

"We pitch them."

"You throw them out?"

"That's right. Every last bit."

"Could I have them?"

"Pardon me, ma'am, but what would you want with a hundred leftover petit fours and cucumber sandwiches?"

"I know some people who need them. Hungry people."

His face, suspicious until now, relaxed into a smile. "You can have all you want.

I'll even help you pack 'em up. You some kind of social worker or something?"

"Something like that. I'm a minister."

"No kidding? Hey, that's pretty cool."

"This won't get you into trouble, will it?" she asked as they stacked food into boxes.

"Can't think why. I'm glad to see the food go to folks who need it. I never could feel right about tossing out good food. Not when there're folks who're hungry."

Carla stuck out her hand. "Carla Stevens. And you're —"

"Chuck Sanders. The missus here, she call me Charles. But it's just plain Chuck."

"I'm pleased to meet you, Chuck."

"Same here, ma'am."

Sam had kept silent up until now, content to watch Carla work her magic on the man. Now he introduced himself. "Sam Hastings."

Chuck gave him a long look. "Say, aren't you the guy that just got himself elected to City Council?"

"Guilty as charged."

"You helping the lady here?"

"I guess I am."

Chuck grinned. "I voted for you. Maybe you're going to work out all right."

They worked quickly, filling a dozen or

so boxes. When they'd finished, Carla pressed a quick kiss to Chuck's cheek. "I can't thank you enough."

"Don't thank me, ma'am. I'm just glad to see the food going somewhere it's needed."

"It will," she assured him. She turned to Sam. "You don't have to leave. I'll call a cab and —"

"I'm going with you. You plan on taking this down to the shelter tonight, right?"

"They could use it. Each night, more and more people show up hungry. There's never enough food to go around."

"You never stop, do you?"

"I can't help what I am, Sam."

"No, I don't guess you can. That's why I love you."

Chapter Eight

"You what?"

"That's why I love you." He grabbed her hand. "We've got a delivery to make."

"You can't say something like that and then leave it."

"Something like what?"

"Something like 'I love you.' "

"Why not? It's the truth." He brushed his lips against hers.

"Sam —"

"I know. This isn't the right place. Or the right time. The story of our relationship." He began carrying boxes of food out the kitchen door.

After they'd filled his truck with petit fours, finger sandwiches, and hors d'oeuvres, Sam made his apologies to his hosts.

He didn't regret leaving the party early. He'd felt stifled there, surrounded by people who talked too much and thought too little.

"You can let me out here," Carla said when he pulled up in front of the shelter.

"Uh-uh. I'm staying."

Together, they unloaded the food from his truck and took it inside. The coordinator greeted them.

"Is that what I think it is?" he asked.

Carla nodded. "I thought you might need it."

"Do we ever. Twenty more people arrived tonight. We ran out of food over two hours ago. I was just about to go out and see what I could find." He kissed Carla's cheek. "You're a lifesaver — you and your friend."

Sam stuck out his hand. "Sam Hastings. Glad we could help."

"Tom Beringer."

Sam started to unbutton his coat when Tom stopped him.

"You'll probably want that."

For the first time, Sam noticed the cold. "Can't you turn up the heat?"

Tom and Carla exchanged looks.

"New at this, aren't you?" Tom asked.

"You could say that," Sam agreed. "But that doesn't answer my question."

"There's not enough money to heat the building all night," Carla said. "They turn down the heat after ten and turn it up again in the morning."

"That's crazy. It's thirty degrees out. And getting colder."

Tom sighed. "Yeah. But who said we lived in a sane world?" He began opening up the bags of food and gave a low whistle. "What did you two do? Crash a society party and then make off with all the food?"

Sam grinned. "Something like that."

For the first time, Tom seemed to notice their clothes. "You weren't kidding, were you? What kind of shindig are you dressed for?"

"We were at a party celebrating Sam's election to City Council," Carla said.

Tom looked at Sam with new interest. "I hope you plan to do something about this." He waved his hands to include the room, the people.

Sam gave him a level look. "I plan to."

The coordinator turned his attention back to the food. "Our people are in for a treat tonight. I only wish you'd brought some coffee or soup. It'd help take the chill out."

Sam looked at the array of tiny sandwiches, cakes, and cookies. They were bits of fluff. These people needed real food. It was too late now to do anything about it, but that was going to change.

In the main room of the shelter, Tom said a few words, and the people gathered around him. "Reverend Stevens, would you lead us in prayer?" he asked.

160

A hush fell over the room, the silence broken only by the whimper of a baby as Carla offered a blessing upon the food. Sam found himself listening to the words, impressed by their simplicity. Murmured "amens" followed the prayer.

The people began to file in line. He marveled at the quiet taking of places. There was no pushing or shoving, such as he'd experienced at sporting events or concerts he'd attended. Instead, children and elderly people were encouraged to go first.

"Sam, can you hand out the sandwiches?" Tom asked. "Jeannie here will help you." He pointed to a teenage girl who smiled shyly.

"Sure." Sam felt awkward at first placing the tiny sandwiches upon plates, but he and Jeannie soon developed a rhythm.

"Do you volunteer here often?" he asked.

She gave him an odd look. "I *live* here."

He felt like he'd been kicked in the gut. He stole another look at the girl. She was pretty, with light-brown hair, turned-up nose, and green eyes. Her clothes were worn but clean. She looked like any other teenager. She *was* any other teenager — except that she lived in a shelter.

"How long?" he asked.

"A couple of weeks. I was living on the street until she —" Jeannie pointed to Carla. "— gave me a card with this address."

"Do you like it?" he asked and then silently kicked himself. If he'd ever asked a more stupid question in his life, he wasn't aware of it. But he wanted to know. He *needed* to know.

She shrugged. "It's not bad. Better than the streets. Better than home."

It was the last that made him wince.

"How did you —"

"Enough with the questions, okay?"

"Sure. I'm sorry."

"Yeah, well, so am I. So are a lot of people. But it doesn't change anything."

No, it didn't change a thing, Sam realized. His sympathy was as useless as were the empty words mouthed by city leaders who were more interested in vote-getting than in helping.

"Better get ready," Jeannie said. "They're coming."

Sam looked up to see the line of people approaching them. He speeded up his pace until several dozen plates filled the table.

"Thank you, mister," a small girl said as Sam handed her a plate of food.

He hunkered down to her level. "You're welcome. What's your name?"

"Sarah. What's yours?"

"I'm Sam." He reached out to smooth back a wisp of hair that had escaped her ponytail.

"I'm glad you and the pretty lady came. Is she your wife?"

Sam looked over to where Carla was holding a baby so that a woman — probably the child's mother — could wait in line. "No," he said softly, "she's not my wife."

"She's nice," Sarah said. "She gave me this." Sarah opened her hand to reveal a gleaming penny. "Isn't it pretty?"

"Very pretty," he agreed, his gaze still on Carla. He watched as she nuzzled the baby close to her. For a moment, he allowed himself to imagine Carla holding *their* baby. She'd be a great mother.

"I'd better go now," Sarah said, drawing his attention back to her. "Or my mommy will get worried."

"Where is your mother?"

"Over there." Sarah pointed to a woman standing far back from the crowd of people waiting in line for food.

"Isn't she going to have something to eat?"

163

Sarah shook her head. "She said she wasn't hungry. But I think she is. She hasn't had anything to eat since yesterday morning."

"Excuse me," Sam whispered to Jeannie. "I'll be back in a minute."

He picked up a plate of food, all the while wishing he had something more substantial to offer than finger sandwiches and iced cakes. He made his way through the crowd of people until he found the pale woman Sarah had identified as her mother. She looked ready to drop, but she held herself with quiet dignity, her arms folded across her chest, her head high. The thin sweater she wore was scant protection against the cold, and Sam wondered if she'd accept his coat if he offered it. Somehow, he doubted it.

"I thought you might like this," he said, offering the plate to her instead.

She gave him a tired smile. "Thank you. But I'm not very hungry."

"There's plenty," he said gently.

"All these children —" She gestured around her. "— they need it more. I'll wait."

"You need to keep up your strength if you're going to take care of Sarah." At her astonished look, he smiled. "I met Sarah.

You have a beautiful daughter. You must be very proud of her."

The woman's eyes, eyes that looked too old for her slight body and braided hair, brightened momentarily. "I am. She's the one good thing in my life."

"Then you have to take care of yourself. For her." Again, he extended the plate of food.

He must have touched a chord for she nodded and accepted it. "Thank you. You're very kind."

"No, but I know someone who is." His gaze drifted to Carla who was still rocking the baby.

"She's lovely."

"Yes," he said quietly, "she is."

Balancing her plate and cup of water carefully, Sarah joined her mother. "Thank you, mister. My mommy was hungry."

Sam watched as mother and daughter found room at the long table. No one complained at making room for two more at the already crowded table. There was an acceptance here that Sam envied, perhaps because it was so simple.

There were no divisions by class or race, occupation or education. These people, all of whom had suffered some kind of blow, had bonded together, offering each other the dignity and respect denied them on the outside.

He retraced his steps and once more took his place beside Jeannie. As he handed out the food, he had to pause several times to brush tears from his eyes.

For the first time, he realized how the lavish celebration party must have seemed to Carla. Trivial. Excessive. And most of all, wasteful. His friends, the ones he'd defended so vehemently, suddenly appeared as plastic as their smiles, with their petty concerns.

He had a lot to learn. He watched as Carla now comforted a small boy who had tripped and dropped his plate of food. But he had a good teacher — a very good teacher. "That's the last of it," Jeannie said.

Sam looked at the empty boxes and sacks. Thank heavens there'd been enough food to go around — this time. What about tomorrow night and the night after that?

He asked the questions of Tom. "What about tomorrow? Will there be food?"

Tom gave Sam a long look. What Sam saw in the coordinator's eyes startled him: pity. Not for the people, but for him.

"There'll be some. Trucks from the food

bank drop off canned goods twice a week."

"What about bread, eggs, milk?"

"We have volunteers who pick up day-old items from the stores."

"Will there be enough?" Sam persisted.

"There's never enough. But we'll make do." Tom smiled grimly. "We have to."

Once again, Sam was reminded of how little he knew and how much he had to learn.

"When's it going to change?"

"That depends, Sam."

"On what?"

"On you. Me. Carla. And the rest of the people out there."

"One person . . . one voice," Sam murmured. "Maybe it really does start there."

Tom looked at him with approval.

"I guess the trick is convincing more people to care," Sam said, thinking aloud.

"You got it." Tom slapped him on the back. "Now comes the fun part."

Sam turned an inquiring look to Carla, who had joined them.

"Cleanup," she explained.

He barely stifled a groan. He was exhausted. They'd been serving food for the last couple of hours without a break.

"If you'd rather go home, I can hitch a ride with someone," she said.

Sam looked at the lines of exhaustion and strain etched in her face. She had to be at least as tired as he was. "No way. I'm in for the long haul."

Carla squeezed his arm and gave him a look of such warmth that he squirmed, knowing he didn't deserve it. "My hero," she said playfully.

"Don't."

"Don't what?"

"Don't make me out to be something that I'm not. I'm afraid I'm more like my friends than I realized. I'm selfish, short-sighted, and —"

She put a finger to his lips. "You're nothing like them. You care about people. I saw you with that little girl and her mother. I also saw you slip some money into her pocket."

At one time he would have been embarrassed at having someone witness such an act, but not with Carla. They'd come too far for that. "She needed it."

"I know." Carla brushed his cheek with her hand. "I'm sorry I took you from the party, but I'm glad you came with me."

"So am I," he said softly.

At home, he remembered the questions he'd posed to Tom and later to Carla. Questions like, what happened the next

time a cold spell hit, flooding the shelter
with more people than they were equipped
to handle? Questions like, what happened
when the food ran out? Questions like,
where would Sarah and her mother sleep
tomorrow night?

The questions badgered him through the
night because he had no answers.

Carla shifted the bouquet of mums to
her other arm and pressed the doorbell.

The whine of a small motor drowned
out the sound, and she tried again.
Finally, she pushed on the door, finding it
open. She sighed as she walked inside.
How many times had she told Maude and
Ethan they needed to keep their door
locked?

A smile crept past her exasperation as
she remembered Maude's retort: "Friends
know they're welcome. If it's not a friend,
then we'd better make one of him."

"Maude? Ethan? It's Carla."

There was still no answer.

She was able to identify the noise now —
a power saw ripping into wood. She followed the sound into the kitchen where
she found Maude, Ethan, and . . . Sam.
What was he doing here?

"Goodness, Carla, we didn't hear you

above all this racket," Maude said. She tapped Sam on the arm.

He switched off the saw, raised his protective goggles, and grinned at Carla.

"Sit, sit," Maude ordered, backing up her wheelchair to make room for Carla at the table. "Ethan, clear off that chair for the Reverend."

"That's all right," Carla said. "I just wanted to drop these by and say welcome home, but I can see you're busy."

Ethan slapped Sam on the back. "Sam here volunteered to widen the doorways and put up ramps so Maude can get around."

Carla looked at Sam, not caring that the love she felt showed plainly in her face. "That's thoughtful of you."

He shrugged, clearly uncomfortable with being the center of attention. "It needed to be done. Besides, I think I got a pretty good deal. Maude's invited me for Sunday dinner next week."

"That's right," Maude said proudly. "I may be in this thing for a while, but I can still take care of my menfolk." She wheeled over to pat Sam's hand. "Sam's one of the family." She looked at the flowers in Carla's hands. "How did you know I love mums? Ethan, get a vase for those."

Awkwardly, Ethan stuffed the flowers into a mason jar.

Maude rolled her eyes. "Trust a man to stuff flowers into a canning jar when there's a perfectly good vase in the cupboard."

"I like canning jars," Ethan said. "Reminds me of your homemade jelly."

During the exchange, Sam had walked over to stand behind Carla and rested his hands on her shoulders. He dipped his head, his breath fanning her cheek.

"Can you stay?" Ethan asked Carla. "We were going to have lunch in a few minutes. I'm cooking today — franks and beans."

"Not today," she said regretfully. "I've got visits to make. Maybe another time."

"I'll see you to the door," Sam said, taking her hand.

Carla looked up in time to see the smiles Ethan and Maude exchanged.

"You're a nice man, Sam Hastings," she said as they walked through the hallway to the front door.

"It's not a big deal. They needed help making the house wheelchair-accessible so Maude could come home. Anyone would have done the same thing."

"Not anyone, Sam. Only someone who cared. Only someone like you." She sensed

171

his discomfort at her praise and changed the subject. "I didn't know you knew your way around power tools."

"I put myself through school working at construction sites in the summers. I even thought about a career in it, but I decided I liked designing things better than building them."

"But your parents —"

"Are my parents, not my meal ticket."

"I'm sorry. I didn't mean —"

"It's all right. A lot of people make the same mistake. I may have been born with a silver spoon in my mouth, but that doesn't mean it stayed there."

"No, it doesn't. You never talk about your parents much."

He lifted a shoulder. "There's not much to say. We . . . aren't close."

She heard the careful indifference in his voice, an indifference that she suspected masked a very real pain. She turned away, knowing he wouldn't appreciate the tears she felt prick her eyes. Sam's arms came around her, pulling her against him. She let her head drop into the hollow of his shoulder.

They stayed that way until she turned in his arms, slipping her hands behind his neck.

"You're a special kind of man." She stroked her palm down his cheek. It was rough with stubble, creating a pleasant friction against her hand. "Thank you."

"For what?"

"For being who you are. What you are."

"What am I?"

The man I love. But she didn't say the words aloud. She needed privacy for that. Right now, she wanted to hug the words to her, savor them. She touched her lips to his.

"Thanks again for what you're doing for Maude and Ethan."

Sam watched as she walked down the path to her car. He put a finger to his lips, still warm from her kiss.

"No, Carla," he said softly, "thank you. For teaching me how to care."

He spent the rest of the day installing ramps and handrails for Maude. The house was small, cramped, and crowded with pictures and memories, a world apart from the white-columned mansion where he'd grown up.

But it was more of a home than the mansion would ever be. It had probably never seen a professional decorator. Sam had an idea that Maude and Ethan would scoff at the idea of someone else choosing the things that surrounded them.

His mother had routinely redecorated the house every other year, each version as cold and sterile as the last, each designed to impress rather than to comfort, none designed with a small boy in mind.

The Sandbergs' home radiated love, but Sam knew the love would be there no matter where they lived. Their love for each other was a palpable thing and wrapped itself around whoever came into contact with it.

When he finished, Ethan and Maude thanked him profusely.

"If it wasn't for you, I don't know what we'd have done," Ethan admitted. "When the doctor said Maude couldn't come home because of the wheelchair. . . ." He turned away and blew his nose.

"Neither do I," Maude seconded, taking Sam's hand and squeezing it. "If I couldn't have come back to my own home. . . ." Her voice faltered, and she sniffled. "I don't know what I'd have done. Thank you for making it happen."

Touched by the tears she didn't bother to wipe away, Sam bent over to plant a kiss on Maude's cheek. "I liked doing it," he said and knew it was true.

"Don't you forget Sunday dinner, you hear?" she reminded him as he gathered up his tools. "I'm making fried chicken, mashed potatoes, and gravy."

"I'm counting on it." He shook hands with Ethan and kissed Maude once more.

Driving home, he smiled, remembering Maude and Ethan's gratitude for what had been a small thing. He was beginning to understand what Carla had tried to tell him: helping others gave meaning to life. Until he'd met her, he hadn't understood that.

His life had been full, but aside from work, meaningless. The round of parties and social affairs he'd once enjoyed had turned flat, until he'd felt he was only going through the motions of pretending to have a good time.

It had taken Carla to turn his life around.

"The downtown shelter needs more funds," Sam said, warming to his subject at his first official meeting as a council member. "As the weather turns colder, the shelter's getting more people every night. They can't operate without money."

"Sam, Sam." Pete Hammond smiled genially. "We'd all like to be able to budget more money for the shelter. I think I speak for everyone here when I say we all feel sorry for those people." He looked around the oval table at the other members of the council and was rewarded with a chorus of murmured assents.

"But money's tight. I don't have to tell you that. You're a businessman. You know the realities."

Sam knew the realities only too well. He'd seen them, felt them, tasted them last night. Realities like no heat after ten p.m. Realities like not enough food. Realities like too many people and too few beds.

He checked the impatient words that threatened to escape. His first meeting as a city councilman was not going well. He'd manage to antagonize Pete Hammond, one of his chief supporters, and several other members as well.

He had to try one more time. "If you'd visit the shelter, Pete, you'd see what I mean."

Pete narrowed his eyes. "You're sounding like that lady minister you brought to my house. That's all well and fine for someone like that. But you've got to maintain some objectivity."

"While we're being objective, there are people going hungry."

"Sam, this being your first time and all, it might be wise if you sat back and listened," Pete said. His voice was mild, but his eyes were hard. "You might pick up on some pointers."

Sam caught the looks being passed about. If he wasn't careful, he'd destroy any chance he had of making a difference. He'd bide his time, but he didn't intend to remain silent forever.

He listened as the council discussed the other issues on the agenda. Only when the meeting broke up did Pete turn to him.

"You're bright, Sam. Too bright to be making enemies your first day." The warning was unmistakable.

"Sorry," Sam said briefly. "I didn't mean to offend anyone."

Pete smiled. "No offense taken. You'll learn the ropes soon enough."

Sam had a feeling he might be learning more than he ever wanted to. He'd learned an important lesson today. If he wanted the council to do something, he had to present it in a way they understood. And that meant appealing to their business sense. The bottom line was just as real in running the city as in running a business.

He gathered up his papers and headed to

the bank of elevators on the fourth floor of the city building. He had a couple of calls to make.

Chapter Nine

"We found it! The perfect piece of property. Right here in Saratoga."

Carla threw herself into Sam's arms. He twirled her around and around until they were both dizzy.

"It's perfect, absolutely perfect. It's —"

"Hold on." He curved an arm around her shoulders and led her over to the leather couch in his office. "Slow down and take a deep breath. It's not going anywhere, is it?"

She frowned. "That's the part we're not sure about. Some other organization has their eye on it, so we have to act fast. The city has to approve it, of course. Then we have to make our bid. And then —"

Sam kissed her. "And then you have to let me take you out to dinner to celebrate."

"There's no time. There's too much to do."

He kissed her again. "We'll make time. For everything. Now tell me all about it."

He listened while Carla filled him in on the details of the proposed property for the

Community Home. When she told him its location, he frowned. Something niggled at the back of his mind before he identified what it was. Another organization, The High Plains Art Council, had already earmarked the property as a possible site for a sculpture garden. That wasn't insurmountable, though.

Sam was more concerned with the location. It didn't have access to public transportation and was far removed from schools and shopping centers, three strikes against it already.

Tell her.

She'll understand.

Why spoil her excitement until you know for sure that the location isn't right?

It'll be easier in the long run if you tell her about your doubts now.

The inner conversation played over and over in his mind until he wasn't sure of anything. The only thing he knew was he couldn't lose Carla.

He'd research the property. If the report came up negative, there'd be time enough to break the bad news to her later.

Coward.

He appeased his conscience with the reminder that he didn't know the property would be unsuitable. He had only his suspicions.

Carla kept talking, oblivious to his growing concern. That was the way he wanted it for right now. If his fears were groundless, there'd be no problem. If, however, they weren't . . .

He let the thought go unfinished, unwilling to pursue it now.

Carla's voice broke into his thoughts. "You'll support it, won't you, Sam?"

He took his time in answering, choosing his words carefully. "If the research shows the property is right for the Community Center, I'll support it with everything I've got."

"See? You aren't like the rest. You care. You really care."

"I care, Carla."

When she lifted her lips to his, he kissed her. When his lips met hers, he pushed away the last of his doubts. Carla had worked too hard to make her dream come true. He wouldn't — he *couldn't* — be the one to destroy it. Not without cause.

He loved her too much.

Pete Hammond stuck his head in Sam's office at the city building. "Sam, got a minute?"

"Sure. Come on in."

Inwardly, Sam groaned. The last thing

he wanted was another bit of friendly advice from Pete on "learning the ropes." Pete's advice usually consisted of the importance of being a team player, but translated as "don't make waves."

"It's this proposal for the site for the community home," Pete said, throwing down a file on Sam's desk.

"What about it?"

"It's not going to work."

"Why not?"

"Look at the preliminary report and tell me what you think."

Sam scanned the file. Whatever he might think of Pete, he couldn't fault the concise report in front of him. Location to schools, public transportation, and shopping centers made the site Carla's group proposed a poor choice, just as Sam had feared.

"See what I mean?" Pete demanded.

Sam loosened his tie and undid the top button of his shirt. It had already been a long day. It promised to get longer. "I see what you mean."

"We decided to go ahead with the vote today. You'll be there?"

"Yeah, I'll be there."

Pete hesitated, looking unsure of himself for the first time. "You still seeing that lady minister?"

Sam gave a brief nod.

"She feels pretty strongly about the community home, doesn't she?"

"She's worked toward it for a long time."

"Might make it sort of rough on you."

"If you're asking if that'll affect how I do my job, then you don't know me very well." Sam didn't bother to disguise the coolness in his tone.

"Didn't mean to offend you, boy," Pete said. "I know you'll do the right thing."

Sam stayed in his office another hour, trying to find a way around the problem of making the proposed site right for the community home. But the facts hadn't changed, no matter how much he might want them to. He pushed his chair back from his desk. He didn't like it, but he knew what he had to do.

Two hours later, he stepped out of the council room, knowing he'd done the only thing he could. Only how did he tell Carla that he'd voted against something she'd worked so hard for?

Admit it, Hastings. You're a coward. A first-class coward who's afraid to face the woman you love.

He busied himself in his office, writing letters that could have waited, reading reports he'd already read. But he couldn't put it off forever.

The drive to Carla's house took less time than he'd hoped.

"I didn't expect you tonight," she said as she let him inside. She laced her arms around his neck and lifted her face for a kiss.

Sam gently freed himself from her embrace and started to pace. He needed the distance between them in order to say what he had to.

"Is something wrong?" she asked.

"The Council voted today on the land."

"Great! That means we can start moving on the project even sooner than we hoped. We already have a promise from a major supplier to donate lumber. I'm working on a cement company right now to let us have a truck and materials at cost." She hugged herself and twirled around. "Oh, Sam, it's all coming together. Now all we need —"

His breath caught as she turned to him. She was beautiful, happiness shimmering in her eyes. In that instant, he hated himself for what he had to do.

"Carla, the Council voted against the site."

"I don't understand."

He saw the confusion in her face, the beginnings of pain supplanting the happiness that had been there only seconds before. It was his fault. If he'd told her about his fears in the beginning, he could have saved her a world of disappointment.

"Why did they vote against it? I thought you said it'd pass."

"I said I thought it had a good chance provided the reports came back favorable."

"They didn't?"

He sighed heavily. "No. They showed —"

"Who voted against it?"

"Does it matter?"

Now it was her turn to pace. "Hammond, for sure. And probably Mannering and Wainwright. Didn't you say they're golf buddies?"

"They play golf together," he said. "But that's not why the vote turned out the way it did." He hesitated, trying to find the right words, only there were none. "I'm sorry."

"It's not your fault," she said, crossing the room to stand beside him. "I know you did your best. If only there were more on the City Council like you, we'd have our community home. Now we just have to start over."

Sam looked at her clear blue eyes and knew he couldn't let a lie stand between them, even an unspoken one. "I voted against it."

She didn't speak but only stared at him. When the words came, they were laced with bewilderment and pain. "I don't believe it. You said you believed in what we were doing. You wanted the community home built as much as I did. I know you did."

"I did. I do. But. . . ."

"But what?"

"The research showed —"

"I don't care what the research showed. I only care why you voted against us. Why, Sam? Why?"

"If you'll let me explain —"

"Explain what? Explain why you voted against a project that could help so many people? Explain why you voted against a home for children who have to sleep in the streets? Explain why you voted against everything I believe in?"

Sam took a deep breath, hearing the anguish in her voice and knowing he'd put it there. "You won't believe this, but I was trying to help you and your group."

"You're right, I don't believe it. You must've laughed yourself to sleep at night. What was it, Sam? Sweet-talk the naive little minister, convince her you cared, pretend you believed in the same things she did, and then let her down easy when you got tired of her? The novelty wore off, and you wanted to get back to your own kind."

He flinched under her attack. "It wasn't like that."

"No? Tell me how it was, then."

"You know how it was," he said in a low voice. "I love you, Carla."

"Do you?"

"You know I do. I thought you felt the same."

She turned away.

He grabbed her and spun her around, forcing her to look at him. "I've never said those words to another woman."

"How can you say you love me and then try to destroy everything I believe in?"

"What I feel for you has nothing to do with the community home. And, for the record, I didn't vote against *it*. I voted against that location." He took a deep breath, trying to check the anger that threatened to spill over. If he gave way to it now, they were both lost. "I voted against a piece of property, not you."

"That piece of property is what I've spent the last two years working for."

"That piece of property wasn't suitable for your purposes. But it's not the only land available. We'll find a different site, a better one —"

"There isn't another one," she said, the misery in her voice tearing him apart. "Don't you think we searched for something closer to schools and shopping? This was the best we could come up with, the *only* thing we could come up with in our price range."

"I'll help you. If we work together, we can —"

"No, thanks. We've had enough of your kind of help. We can't afford any more."

"It wasn't the right place for the home," he said in an even tone, barely holding on to his temper. "If you looked at the research, you'd see that for yourself."

Her gaze raked him with cold contempt. "What I see is another politician. Goodbye, Sam."

He started toward her, but she stopped him with only a look. Knowing she needed time to grieve for the loss of her dream, he let himself out.

Sleet pummeled him as he walked to his truck, and he turned up his collar against the cold. He was grateful for the sleet as he drove home. Negotiating the rain-slick roads kept his thoughts at bay.

At home, he started toward the phone

and then stopped himself. He'd give her time. And he'd stay away. But not forever, he promised himself. Not forever.

"It's not over, sweetheart," he said to himself. "Not by a long shot."

When Carla awakened that morning, it took her a few minutes to remember. Then it hit her. Sam was no longer a part of her life.

Sam.

The community home.

Both were gone, and, along with them, her dreams. She shook off her lethargy and forced herself to climb out of bed. She padded into the bathroom, looked in the mirror, and grimaced. Pale cheeks, red-rimmed eyes, and matted hair gave mute evidence of her troubled sleep.

She was still trying to come to grips with what had happened. Part of it seemed surreal, as if it happened to someone else and she was merely a bystander, watching a play unfold.

But the pain in her heart was real enough.

How could I've been so wrong? Dear heaven, how could I have been so wrong?

The question plagued her throughout the day, undermining her confidence, until she longed to huddle in a miserable heap. But she had visits to make, a Bible study group to lead, a sermon to prepare.

The day set the pattern for those to come. She pushed her way through them by sheer force of will. And if, in the privacy of her home, she gave way to the heartache that was never far away, no one knew.

When a week passed, Carla acknowledged that she still loved Sam, despite everything. She'd always believed that love was enough to endure any hardship.

She'd been wrong.

She hadn't been sleeping well. Strike that — she hadn't been sleeping at all. Memories of the scene in her living room haunted her nights, making sleep impossible. They invaded the daylight hours also, until she was no longer sure which was which.

Now, she could barely summon enough energy to eat breakfast. She picked at the toast and eggs she'd forced herself to make with little enthusiasm.

They tasted as flat as she felt.

Resolutely, she started eating. *One bite at a time,* she reminded herself. *One step at a time.*

It had become her motto for getting through the days. Some days were better than others. She'd taken on more volunteer work, determined to fill the hours until she was too tired to think or feel. But her strategy had backfired. She was tired, all right, close to exhaustion, but it didn't make sleep come any more easily.

The pain had mercifully blunted to a dull ache. It didn't rip her apart as she'd feared it might. Instead, it had settled around her heart with depressing heaviness.

She wanted to cry, had tried to cry, but the tears wouldn't come, no matter how hard she wished they would. Tears would be a release from the pain that lodged in her heart.

Perhaps, she reflected, there was a grief so intense that nothing could erase it.

Her spirits lifted for a moment as she remembered this was her day to volunteer at the preemie unit of the hospital.

Two hours later, she held six-week-old Joshua Martin. His tiny fist was curved into a ball that he was trying unsuccessfully to suck. His flailing arms made it next to impossible.

"You're getting so big," she crooned, tucking his arms beneath a blue blanket and bundling him close to her. "Pretty soon Mommy and Daddy can take you home."

Even the slightest weight gain was considered cause for celebration for Joshua, whose birth weight was just shy of two and a half pounds. Now he was a whopping four pounds and eating on his own.

The feeding tubes had been removed three days ago. He had just finished two ounces of milk from a bottle, a big step forward for a baby who didn't have the strength to suck at all four weeks ago.

"You'll be wanting a burger and fries before too long," she said, nuzzling him against her cheek. "None of this baby food for a big boy like you."

Joshua wrinkled up his face, turning it even redder than it had been.

"Okay, okay," she soothed. "I get the message. Maybe you're not ready for the big time yet. We'll just stick with formula for now. Right?"

He gurgled, a sound she took for consent.

"Do you need to burp after that big meal?" Gently, she patted his back, her hand completely covering the small surface.

A small but unmistakable burp followed, the sound drawing a smile from her.

"You'll be burping with the best of them soon," she predicted. As she spoke, she checked the disposable diaper loosely fastened around Joshua.

Finding it wet, she scooped his tiny hips up, spread another diaper beneath him, and secured the blue tabs.

Joshua expressed his displeasure at the indignity with a lusty wail. He kicked his legs wildly and screwed up his face into a ball of outrage.

"Sorry about that," she said, disposing of the soiled diaper. "But you'll feel better with a dry bottom."

His sobs had subsided, but he continued to regard her with reproachful eyes.

"You'll just have to trust me on that one," she said.

Her throat tightened as she remembered another time she'd changed a diaper. Sam had been there then, helping her tend Emilie. A sad smile brushed her lips. He'd been nervous at first, but he'd soon adjusted, holding Emilie with endearing awkwardness.

Carla blinked back tears that had chosen now to make their appearance. One slid down her cheek, and she knuckled it away.

A nurse appeared, and Carla regretfully handed Joshua over to her.

"You're a miracle worker, Reverend Stevens," the nurse said. "You got him to finish all his formula. Usually he's good for just an ounce at a time."

"He did it all himself. He even confided to me that he has a hankering for a burger and fries."

The nurse laughed. "If he keeps up this way, he'll be out of here in a couple of more weeks. That's when we really celebrate."

"I hope so," Carla said, stroking Joshua's cheek one more time.

She'd give anything for a child of her own. Resolutely, she pushed that from her mind. The picture of Sam holding Emilie had refused to disappear, and she shook her head to dislodge it.

"We appreciate all you do here," the nurse added, smiling warmly at Carla. "Especially the extra hours you've been putting in this week. Every bit of attention these little guys get makes a difference."

"I like being here," Carla said truthfully, avoiding the topic of her extra hours.

She didn't want praise for what had, after all, been an escape mechanism for her. What better way to fill the empty hours than holding these tiny babies who had upset nature's timetable by being born too early? She watched as the nurse checked Joshua's temperature and pulse and then jotted down the notations on a clipboard.

When she'd started volunteering at the neonatal unit at the hospital, the nurses had cautioned her against getting too involved with the tiny patients. Despite the best care available and a lot of prayers, some of the babies didn't make it. But Carla had never been able to hold back her involvement or her love.

She loved each of the babies there, grieving over the ones who died and rejoicing over the ones who eventually got to go home. She'd sat in on support groups made up of parents of preemies, volunteers, and hospital staff. More than once, she'd comforted bereaved parents whose babies didn't survive, sharing their tears and their grief.

She removed the sterile gown and cap and tossed them into the receptacle for soiled garments. With the high rate of infection in a hospital, it was imperative to keep the preemie unit germ-free.

"See you Thursday," the nurse called after her.

"Thursday," Carla echoed. She checked her watch. It was too late for lunch, too early for dinner. Not that she was particularly hungry.

On an impulse, she stopped at Maude and Ethan's on the way home. They could always cheer her up, and she desperately needed that right now. Just the thought of being around them and witnessing their love for each other lifted her spirits.

As she started to back her compact car into the one remaining parking space on the street, she noticed a truck parked in front of their house — Sam's truck.

Her heart hammered against her ribs. She ached to see him, yet shied away, remembering the angry words she'd tossed at him the last time they'd been together.

She pulled away from the curb and drove home. It didn't surprise her that Sam was visiting Ethan and Maude. He'd told her he felt more at home there than he ever had at the house where he'd grown up. What surprised her was the sense of being excluded that she felt.

Almost angrily, she reminded herself that she had no right to feel that way. Maude and Ethan were certainly entitled to entertain anyone whom they chose in their home. So why did she feel like crying? The answer was simple.

Sam.

Even knowing what she did, she couldn't

help loving him. She had no one to blame but herself. She'd known what she was risking when she became involved with him. She just hadn't known how much it was going to hurt.

She pulled into her driveway and rested her head on the steering wheel. The tears that had started at the hospital now fell freely.

She let them have their way.

The days stumbled over one another, rushing to pile up into weeks until it was almost Thanksgiving. Carla welcomed the extra demands of the holiday season, for they kept her from thinking — and feeling — too much.

Baskets for the poor needed to be filled, a children's play about the first Thanksgiving had to be rehearsed, and a special sermon to be given early Thanksgiving morning had to be written.

A cold spell had pushed more people off the streets and into the shelter. Unfortunately, supplies hadn't kept up with the influx of people. Carla had used the money she'd been saving to have her car repainted to buy groceries.

"You shouldn't have done it," Tom Beringer said, hefting two large boxes of food from her car. "But we need it too much for me to refuse."

She picked up the smaller boxes and followed him into the shelter. "I wish it were more."

"So do I. But everything's appreciated."

They made several more trips until the trunk was empty.

Tom set the last of the boxes on the kitchen counter and turned to her. "Your friend was here yesterday."

Her heart stilled. "Sam?"

"Yeah. Brought by some blankets. Said they were just lying around and he didn't need them. Thing was, they still had the tags on them. I figure he went out and bought them and then was too embarrassed to admit it. Funny kind of guy."

"Yeah. Funny." She swallowed around the lump in her throat.

"Well, we'd better get this put away." Tom started unpacking the boxes.

Automatically, she began filling the cabinets.

"Hey, do you really want to put those in there?" he asked.

"What?" Carla looked down at the carton of eggs in her hand. "Sorry. I guess my mind was somewhere else."

Tom smiled. "I'd say that was a fair guess."

After they finished the job, she stayed to help prepare the noonday meal. When they'd served the shelter's residents, she gave a tired sigh and rolled back her sleeves, preparing to wash dishes. She turned on the water and squirted detergent into the sink. She bit her lip as memories of Sam helping her wash dishes at the church potluck assailed her. He'd looked good even in the ruffled apron.

"Why don't you go on home?" Tom suggested. "You look beat."

"Trying to get rid of me already? Who're you going to find who loves to wash dishes as much as I do?"

Tom didn't respond to her teasing but took her hands from the sudsy water and handed her a towel. "I'm worried about you, Carla. You've been running for the last two weeks, trying to be everywhere at once — here, the hospital, the church."

She shrugged. "There's a lot to be done."

"You can't do everything yourself." He gave her a long, probing look. "When are you going to slow down?"

"I can't," she admitted.

He pulled her into his arms. "That's what I was afraid of. It's him, isn't it? Sam."

She thought about denying it and knew

she couldn't. "How did you know?"

"I saw the way you looked at him. What's more, I saw the way he looked at you. The man loves you."

"You're wrong."

"Am I?"

She nodded against his shoulder.

"How do you feel about him?"

She waited, hoping the words wouldn't come. She didn't want them to be true, believed they couldn't be true, and knew they were. "I love him."

"Then tell him."

"It's not that simple."

"No? Why not?"

"Sam voted against the community home."

"I know."

"You know? How?"

"Did you think that kind of thing was going to remain a secret? Did he tell you why he voted against it?"

She started to shake her head before remembering that Sam had tried to tell her his reasons, but she'd been too upset to listen. "He said something about the location not being right."

"He was right."

She turned to stare at Tom in astonishment. "It was the best site we could find."

"That doesn't mean it was right," Tom said in a calm voice and began to dry the dishes she'd already washed. "It was cut off from transportation, shopping centers, schools, everything our people need."

"That's what Sam said."

"But you didn't believe him."

She thought about it. "No. I wanted the home so much."

"We all do. But it won't do any good if it's not in the right place to help the people who need it."

Sam had said the same thing, she remembered. He'd said a lot of things, but she'd been too hurt to listen.

"You think I was wrong?" she asked.

"I think you lead with your heart instead of your head."

Her mouth curved slightly as she acknowledged the truth of Tom's words.

"Hey," he said, "that's not a bad way to live."

"Maybe. But sometimes it's not very smart."

They finished washing the dishes, both careful to keep to safe subjects.

She thought about Tom's words far into the night. Had she been too quick to condemn Sam without hearing him out? Had she worked so long toward her goal that she'd blinded herself to everything and everyone else?

The questions chipped away at her until she no longer knew what was right. She only knew that she loved Sam. But was it too late for them?

Chapter Ten

"Hey, Sam, we need your input."

Guiltily, Sam looked up from where he was doodling on a printed agenda of the City Council meeting. He shook himself out of the blue funk he'd fallen in and turned to Pete Hammond.

"Sorry, Pete. You were saying?"

Someone chuckled. "What's the matter, Sam? Woman trouble?"

"Why don't we keep to business?" Sam returned evenly. "What's up?"

"There's an abandoned warehouse on the corner of Cherry and Madison," Pete Hammond said. "We've got to make a decision on it. Developers want it demolished and the land zoned for residential building. Right now, the city owns it — default on back taxes."

Sam studied the report Pete placed in front of him. He scanned the papers with little interest until he noticed the location. Something clicked in his brain, a breath of an idea that inched its way through the fog he'd been operating under for the past weeks.

"You say the city owns it?" he asked slowly.

"Yeah. Right now it's a white elephant. Not to mention an eyesore."

"I might have an idea," Sam said.

"Well, let's have it." Pete folded his arms across his chest.

"Can you give me a day? Maybe two. I want to do some checking before I stick my neck out."

"Sure. Only don't make it any longer than that. We've got to make a decision on this and get back to the developers. I'm favoring going along with them. All those houses would give us an increased tax base."

Sam tried to focus on the remaining items on the agenda for the rest of the meeting, but his mind kept drifting back to the report on the warehouse. It was crazy, he told himself. Certifiably crazy.

There'd be all sorts of obstacles. Zoning problems, not to mention complaints from the developers who wanted to turn the land into a high-priced subdivision.

But his step was light as he walked outside to his car an hour later.

Six hours later, Sam shoved the papers back and stretched. He'd spent the afternoon at the city building poring over building permits and regulations. Grabbing a hamburger on the way home, he'd eaten while hunched over a sheaf of reports on the warehouse, but he had what he wanted.

The warehouse could be converted into a community home at a cost less than Carla's group had originally estimated. With proximity to schools, shopping centers, and bus lines, it was a natural. Now all he had to do was to convince the rest of the Council that the project made sense — dollars and cents, that is.

He knew how their minds worked. If a project couldn't meet the demands of their bottom line, they weren't interested. He didn't blame them. They were responsible for taxpayer dollars.

He'd scored one victory since he'd been serving on the Council. After marshalling his facts and figures, he'd convinced the others to allocate more funds for the shelter. The problems were a long way from being solved, but at least now there'd be heat during the nights and a few more deliveries of food.

A dozen times, he'd picked up the phone, intending to call Carla. But something had stopped him: pride. He was honest enough to admit he suffered from an excess of it. She hadn't trusted him enough, and it had hurt. But he'd learned something in the last weeks — pride was a lonely companion. He loved Carla, and he knew she loved him. Only one problem remained: convincing her of it.

"A what?" Pete Hammond demanded the following day as Sam outlined his plans for turning the warehouse into a community home for the city's homeless.

"Shut up, Pete," one of the other councilmen said good-naturedly. "Let Sam have his say."

"I factored what it would cost to demolish the warehouse compared with what it would cost to convert it into apartments. We'll spend more money originally, but we'll recoup it and at the same time provide a home for fifty families."

Sam spent the next hour convincing the other members of the Council that his plan made sense.

"Sounds like it could work," Pete said cautiously at the end of Sam's presentation. "Good work."

"Thanks," Sam said, trying unsuccessfully to hide his elation. He made the appropriate noises as the other council members filed past, but his mind was elsewhere.

The next day was Thanksgiving. She didn't know it yet, but he planned on spending it with Carla.

Carla looked around the shelter's kitchen in satisfaction. The spicy scent of sausage competed with the equally spicy scent of *frijoles.* Black-eyed peas sat side by side with potato pancakes.

There'd be Thanksgiving here. Maybe not the most traditional feast in the world, but one that reflected the different backgrounds of the residents.

On the center of the counter sat five turkeys, furnished by the congregation of her church.

"Reverend Stevens, you here?" a voice called from the dining hall.

Carla pushed through the swinging doors of the kitchen and saw Maude and Ethan.

"We've come to help," Maude announced.

"That's right," Ethan hefted two boxes. "We thought you might need a couple of extra pairs of hands. And Maude made some of her pumpkin pies."

Carla sniffed appreciatively. The smell of pumpkin, cinnamon, and cloves filled the room.

"Just show us what needs doing." Maude was already wheeling herself down the narrow aisles between the tables.

"You're both wonderful, but you ought to be home relaxing, watching the parade on TV."

Maude fixed her with a stern look. "Thanksgiving is about sharing, not sitting on your duff and watching life when we could be living it. Ethan and I have a lot to be thankful for this year." She reached for her husband's hand, and finding it, brought it to her cheek.

For a moment, only a moment, Carla allowed herself to remember a time when she'd done the same thing with Sam. She shook away the memory and focused on the present.

"We still have to set the tables, carve the turkey, and make the punch."

"Ethan's a world-class turkey carver," Maude said. "And if you put the dishes and silverware here on the tables, I'll arrange them." Without missing a beat, she added, "Sam stopped by a couple of days ago."

Carla busied herself by rearranging a centerpiece that needed no attention. "Oh?"

Maude eyed her shrewdly. "Seemed

awful lonely. Said you and he weren't seeing each other again."

Carla twisted a napkin until it shredded in her fingers. "We decided we weren't right for each other."

"Hogwash. That man loves you. Any fool can see it."

"We're too different."

"That's good."

"Good?"

Maude nodded emphatically. "Being different is always good. It's when you're too much alike that causes problems. Take Ethan and me. He's on the quiet side, and I'm apt to be a mite talkative." She paused, inviting Carla to share a smile with her. "Wouldn't do at all if we both wanted to talk all the time or we were both quiet as church mice."

"No, I guess it wouldn't," Carla murmured.

"See?" Maude demanded triumphantly. "Different is good. So what's the problem between you and Sam?"

Carla sighed, knowing Maude wouldn't budge until she had an answer. "Sam voted against the community home. Even knowing what it meant to me, he voted against it."

"Did he say why?"

"He said something about it not being the right location."

"Maybe he was right."

Carla felt like she'd been kicked in the gut. That was the second time in two days she'd heard the same thing. She'd expected Maude, of all people, to understand how she felt and back her up.

"How can you say that?"

"Because I know you." Maude speared her with an unflinching gaze. "When you believe in something, you go full speed ahead. Right?"

Carla nodded reluctantly. "What's wrong with that?"

"Nothing . . . if it doesn't blind you to the facts." Maude patted Carla's hand. "You'd be the best one to decide that."

Carla was still reeling under Maude's gentle censure when the old woman startled her once more.

"You have a lot of love to give — to me, Ethan, church members, the preemies at the hospital, all the people here at the shelter. Don't you think it's time you shared some of it with Sam? That man loves you, honey."

Carla barely had a moment to think about that when Maude asked, "What does Sam do when he believes in something?"

"He goes after it —" Carla stopped, frowning.

Hadn't she been attracted to Sam in the first place because he fought for what he believed?

She'd been so sure she was right. But, a niggling voice asked, hadn't Sam been equally sure he was right? Had she asked him to choose between what he believed and her?

"He goes after what he thinks is right," she said at last.

Maude only smiled. "Maybe you two have more in common than you thought."

Carla's hand trembled, and the cider she was pouring spilled onto the paper table-cloth.

"Here," Maude said, blotting up the liquid with a napkin.

Carla tried to keep her mind on what she was doing, but her thoughts kept returning to Sam. She was setting out plates of dev-iled eggs, stuffed celery, and carrot sticks when she saw him.

Dressed in chinos and a navy sweater, he looked more handsome than ever. He also looked a bit unsure of himself.

"What are you doing here?" she asked, then flushed at her less-than-gracious tone.

"Helping you, I hope."

She looked at him, really looked at him, and saw the fine lines etched along his brow and bracketing his mouth. The last two weeks hadn't been easy for him either, she realized.

Sam took the tray from her and finished setting out the appetizers.

He rolled up his sleeves. "Tell me what needs to be done."

"You . . . uh, could help Maude and Ethan serve."

Carla was aware of Maude and Ethan's approving looks as Sam joined them behind the huge serving table. She thought she saw Ethan give him a thumbs-up sign but decided she must've been mistaken.

Tom Beringer pronounced the blessing on the food and invited everyone to get in line. Carla and Tom kept the bowls and platters filled while Sam, Ethan, and Maude dished out the food. Carla glanced up one time to find Sam watching her. Flustered, she ran her fingers through her hair to push it back from her forehead, aware she must look hot and disheveled.

Finally, all the shelter's residents had been served.

Carla sank down on a chair and sighed. "I don't know about the rest of you, but

I'm starved. What do you say we fill our plates and —"

"Sorry," Maude interrupted. "Ethan and I've got other plans."

Carla watched as Maude and Ethan exchanged guilty looks. "Can't you stay for a few minutes? It won't take long."

But Ethan was already pushing Maude's wheelchair down an aisle between tables and waving over his shoulder. "See you later," he called.

"Oh, well." Carla turned to Tom and Sam. "The rest of us can still enjoy Thanksgiving dinner. I think there's even some of Maude's pie left."

Tom checked his watch. "I've got to go too." He looked around, anywhere but at her. "Don't worry about cleaning up. I've got some volunteers coming in to do that."

She felt her self-assurance slipping as she was left alone with Sam in the small kitchen. "I'll just fix us some plates, and we can —"

He took her hand. "We've got some talking to do first."

"But the food —"

"We'll find something along the way." He picked up her coat and draped it over her shoulders.

"On the way? On the way where?" she

asked as she pushed her arms through the sleeves.

"You'll see."

"What are we going to find open on Thanksgiving?" She was tired, hungry, and feeling out of sorts. Ethan, Maude, even Tom had taken off with hardly a good-bye. She'd planned on having Thanksgiving dinner with them. Also, she admitted to herself, she wanted them around to act as a buffer between her and Sam.

"I don't want hamburgers on Thanksgiving," she said, sounding cross. "I want turkey and dressing and potatoes and gravy and pumpkin pie."

Sam hustled her out the back door and bundled her into his truck. He turned on the heater as she fastened her seat belt.

His shoulder brushed hers as he shifted into gear. She found his quiet strength as exciting as before. She loved this man. Whatever he'd done, whatever his reasons, she loved him. She couldn't deny it any longer.

"We might be able to arrange that," he said.

"I don't want to eat Thanksgiving dinner in a restaurant," she said, knowing she sounded cross and not caring. "I wanted to eat it with my friends."

"You know what? You talk a lot. Now, be quiet before I forget that I love you."

"You love me?"

"I'll always love you. Don't you know that?"

Sam leaned across the seat. Carla tried to evade his seeking lips, knowing she'd be lost if he kissed her. But he held her fast. The kiss, as gentle as a summer breeze, broke down her defenses until she relaxed in his arms.

"I should've done this two weeks ago. It always was the best way to communicate with you."

"This doesn't change anything," she said, her voice breathless.

Sam chuckled. "If you don't be quiet, I'll have to do it again."

"But —"

"See what I mean? Some people just don't learn the first time." He kissed her again.

This time she didn't protest — it had been too long. She curled her arms around his neck, no longer caring what had gone before.

"Why? Why did you come?" Her voice broke, and she swallowed back a sob. "I can't bear to send you away again."

"It's going to be all right, sweetheart."

Carla sank back into her seat, unable to

fight him any longer. Whatever he was, she loved him. She watched as he maneuvered through traffic to arrive at an abandoned warehouse.

"If this is some kind of joke —"

"The city doesn't like abandoned buildings," he said conversationally. "In fact, they're considered a real hazard. An insurance nightmare."

"What does that have to do with me?"

"Did you know there are two elementary schools in this district? A bus line runs straight through here. There's also a shopping center within walking distance. A smart architect could probably design it to hold fifty apartments."

"The community home? Oh, Sam, it's perfect — absolutely perfect. How long have you known about it?"

"A couple of days."

"Why didn't you tell me before?"

"I wanted to make sure before I told you. I didn't want you to be disappointed again."

"I'm sorry about what I said," she said, her voice no more than a husky whisper. "You didn't deserve that."

"You were hurting."

"That doesn't excuse what I said. I should've known better. I *did* know better."

"I happen to know of an architectural firm whose owner's a soft touch. He'd probably be willing to design the apartments and give some of the people who will live here a chance to help build it. Who knows, if things work out, maybe he can find full-time work for them."

"Would he?"

He traced the curve of her cheek. "He could be persuaded, given the right encouragement."

"What would that be?"

"He's partial to being kissed by ministers with dark hair and blue eyes."

Her lips found his. "You mean like this?"

"Mmmm. He'll need a lot of encouragement."

She kissed him again.

"Now that we've got that settled, I've got a proposition for you."

"Just what kind of proposition? As a minister, I have to be very careful what kind of proposition I accept."

"It's pretty serious. Are you willing to take on a man who tends to be stubborn, opinionated, and likes his own way?"

"It depends."

"On what?"

"On whether he's willing to take on a

woman who's equally stubborn, opinionated, and likes her own way."

"Oh, he's willing all right. Is there any
hope these two stubborn, opinionated
people can get together?"

"All the hope in the world." Carla punctuated her pronouncement by kissing him
again.

"What about it? Are you willing to take
me on on a permanent basis?"

"I promise full-time devotion to the task."

"You've told me what I have to do . . .
what about you?"

"I promise to love you for the rest of my
life."

"That's one condition I can live with."

Sam pushed open the door to the warehouse.

"Shouldn't that be locked?" Carla asked.

"Probably," he agreed, but he didn't
sound overly concerned.

"Someone's here," she whispered,
hearing scuttling sounds above them. "Do
you think someone's broken in?" She
clutched Sam's arm. "Maybe we should
call the police."

"Let's take a look first. We don't want to
call them on a false alarm."

Sam pushed the button of the freight elevator and took her hand. "Watch your step."

He pulled the handle on the grilled door of the elevator and pushed the button for the second floor. Carla held her breath as the elevator groaned to a start and then wheezed its way to the second floor.

She tugged at his hand. "Sam, I hear something." Even above the noise of the elevator, a racket was audible.

"Then we'd better investigate."

"I love you. You don't have to play hero for me."

He kissed her nose. "I love you too."

"That's not the point," she said impatiently. "You don't know what we'll find up there."

The elevator grumbled to a stop.

"I thought you liked surprises." The door opened, and he pulled her inside.

"Happy Thanksgiving!" The shouted greeting from a dozen or more voices caused her to stop and stare. Tables had been pushed together to form one long table, already set with plates and cutlery.

But it wasn't the tables that drew her attention or the savory aromas coming from the steaming covered dishes. It was the people.

She took an inventory of the smiling faces.

Steve and Marianne Lindquist, with Emilie. Mrs. Miller and the rest of the church ladies plus Mr. Porter. George and friends from the Royal Arms. Mona and Mary Freeman. Tom Beringer. Parents and nurses from the preemie unit at the hospital. In the back were Ethan and Maude.

"How did . . . what are . . . ?" She forced back the tears that threatened to spill over as she kissed each of the people who'd become so dear to her.

"I thought you'd never leave the shelter," Tom said, draping an arm around her shoulders. "We had to break every speed rule in the book to beat you and Sam here."

"That's right," Ethan seconded, pushing Maude's wheelchair next to Carla. "Tom near scared us to death with his driving. But we made it."

"We thought you'd catch on for sure," Maude said. "The look on your face when we said we had to leave . . . you about had me in tears. I almost spilled it then and there."

"You made us feel right bad," Ethan said. "But we knew you'd forgive us when you saw Sam's surprise."

"You knew about this? All of this?"

Maude chuckled. "Sure we did. Sam

told us. Said he needed our help to give you the best Thanksgiving ever."

"We fixed a real old-fashioned Thanksgiving dinner," Mrs. Miller said, hugging Carla and pecking Sam on the cheek. "We'd best be sitting down and commence eating before it gets cold."

The tears would no longer be denied, and Carla's eyes filled as she looked at all her friends — *family,* she corrected herself — crowded in the room.

"Happy Thanksgiving, Carla," Sam said quietly, drawing her into his arms.

"Happy Thanksgiving, Sam."

About the Author

Jane McBride Choate has been weaving stories in her head ever since she can remember, but she shelved her dreams of writing to marry and start a family. After her third child was born, she wrote a short story and submitted it to a children's magazine. To her astonishment, it was accepted. Two children later, she is still creating stories. She believes in the healing power of love, which is why she writes romances. Jane and her husband, Larry, live with their five children in Loveland, Colorado.

We hope you have enjoyed this Large Print book. Other Thorndike, Wheeler or Chivers Press Large Print books are available at your library or directly from the publishers.

For more information about current and upcoming titles, please call or write, without obligation, to:

Publisher
Thorndike Press
295 Kennedy Memorial Drive
Waterville, ME   04901
Tel. (800) 223-1244

Or visit our Web site at:
www.gale.com/thorndike
www.gale.com/wheeler

OR

Chivers Large Print
published by BBC Audiobooks Ltd
St James House, The Square
Lower Bristol Road
Bath BA2 3BH
England
Tel. +44(0) 800 136919
email: bbcaudiobooks@bbc.co.uk
www.bbcaudiobooks.co.uk

All our Large Print titles are designed for easy reading, and all our books are made to last.